G R JORDAN

Mage of the Dice

A Highlands and Islands Detective Thriller #47

First published by Carpetless Publishing 2025

First edition

ISBN (print): 978-1-917497-31-2
ISBN (digital): 978-1-917497-30-5

This book was professionally typeset on Reedsy.
Find out more at reedsy.com

People tend to forget that play is serious

DAVID HOCKNEY, CONTEMPORARY
BRITISH PAINTER

Contents

Foreword

The events of this book, while based around real and also fictitious locations around the UK, are entirely fictional and all characters do not represent any living or deceased person. All companies are fictitious representations and locations have been modified for the purposes of the story. This novel is best read with high dexterity, maximum strength, terrific charisma, and great wisdom. And maybe keep a magic spell or a strange artifact nearby for those dungeon monsters!

Acknowledgments

To Ken, Jean, Colin, Evelyn, John and Rosemary for your work in bringing this novel to completion, your time and effort is deeply appreciated.

Books by G R Jordan

The Highlands and Islands Detective series (Crime)

1. Water's Edge
2. The Bothy
3. The Horror Weekend
4. The Small Ferry
5. Dead at Third Man
6. The Pirate Club
7. A Personal Agenda
8. A Just Punishment
9. The Numerous Deaths of Santa Claus
10. Our Gated Community
11. The Satchel
12. Culhwch Alpha
13. Fair Market Value
14. The Coach Bomber
15. The Culling at Singing Sands
16. Where Justice Fails
17. The Cortado Club
18. Cleared to Die
19. Man Overboard!
20. Antisocial Behaviour
21. Rogues' Gallery
22. The Death of Macleod - Inferno Book 1

Kirsten Stewart Thrillers (Thriller)

1. A Shot at Democracy
2. The Hunted Child
3. The Express Wishes of Mr MacIver
4. The Nationalist Express
5. The Hunt for 'Red Anna'
6. The Execution of Celebrity
7. The Man Everyone Wanted
8. Busman's Holiday
9. A Personal Favour
10. Infiltrator
11. Implosion
12. Traitor

Jac Moonshine Thrillers

1. Jac's Revenge
2. Jac for the People
3. Jac the Pariah

Siobhan Duffy Mysteries

1. A Giant Killing
2. Death of the Witch
3. The Bloodied Hands
4. A Hermit's Death

The Contessa Munroe Mysteries (Cozy Mystery)

1. Corpse Reviver
2. Frostbite
3. Cobra's Fang

The Patrick Smythe Series (Crime)

1. The Disappearance of Russell Hadleigh
2. The Graves of Calgary Bay
3. The Fairy Pools Gathering

Austerley & Kirkgordon Series (Fantasy)

1. Crescendo!
2. The Darkness at Dillingham
3. Dagon's Revenge
4. Ship of Doom

Supernatural and Elder Threat Assessment Agency (SETAA) Series (Fantasy)

1. Scarlett O'Meara: Beastmaster

Island Adventures Series (Cosy Fantasy Adventure)

1. Surface Tensions

Dark Wen Series (Horror Fantasy)

1. The Blasphemous Welcome
2. The Demon's Chalice

Chapter 01

'Why are we all the way out here?' asked the first workman.

'We're out here because this is where we were told to go. Anyway, can you see what it is we're taking up?'

'That's it there—isn't it?'

The first workman looked across what appeared to be a small village green. It wasn't neat enough to be one, but it had all the dimensions. There was a tiny brick structure on the green, and it resembled a poor man's attempt at an oriental house. However, it was too rigid in its dimensions, too exact in its pointing and lacked the artistry and flair that most oriental houses had.

'You think there's much below the ground with it?' asked the second workman.

'I don't know. They told us to bring the digger. So, we've got to dig it up and all around it.'

'Why? I mean, what's it matter out here?'

The first workman looked around him. Mellon Udrigle. Out on the west coast of Scotland. They had to go down poor roads to get here. Ones that weren't that well-travelled. Yes, there would be people who lived out here, who maybe spent most of their time working here, before popping into town

1

occasionally.

But you didn't live out here if you had a city job, office-based, meaning you drove off to Inverness all the time. Instead, you would be based at home, or maybe you were based away on the rigs.

No, this was a place for people who liked to be out in the country, away from everyone, people who didn't like to be disturbed. Well, they were going to be disturbed for a couple of days.

'We've got to do a few other digs in the area. I think they just want to check that there isn't anything further down, below the surface.'

'Like what?' asked the second workman.

'Whatever. Look, Jim, I don't make the rules. I just get given the jobs to do. The first job we're going to do is that little house over there.'

When he said little, the house was maybe up to his knee and certainly wasn't something that he had much of a care for. 'But first thing, Jim,' said the first workman, 'open the flask.'

'We're having coffee already?'

'I've just driven out here. It's taken me a good hour. What, maybe an hour and a half? Blooming right, I'm having coffee.'

The two workmen sat down, opened up their flasks, choosing to stay outside of their vehicle as the weather was warm.

'The joys of the back end of summer.'

'I guess this job doesn't get too exciting in the winter, does it, Davey?'

'No, Jim, it doesn't. So you make the best of days like this that you can. Especially when you're this far from the office. Catch some of the rays.'

Jim's phone began to ring. He looked at his mobile.

'Who's that?'

Davey's phone was also ringing.

'Jim, it's the, er, it's the boss. The trouble out here is, though, the signal's just rubbish.'

The two workmen watched as first one phone rang, and then the other workman's phone rang before eventually giving up for a lack of a response.

'If he asks, you heard nothing, all right?'

Jim nodded. Davey sat and looked again at the surrounding countryside. Most of the berries were gone now, and if the humans hadn't picked them, the birds certainly would have. That was disappointing. He fancied a couple to go with his coffee. About twenty minutes later, he gave that sigh that all workmen do when they have to go back to their job. He licked his lips and put his cup down inside his vehicle.

'You get the digger off the back,' he said to Jim. 'I'm just going to have a check, make sure there's nothing in that wee house, make sure it's easy for us to lift out of the way.'

Jim nodded, and Davey walked across the tatty green. He was dressed in a boilersuit. Well, currently, the top half of it was taken off his shoulders and wrapped tight around his waist. He wasn't missing out on the sun.

As he approached the little house on the green, he put his hand down and in through what could only be described as a window. Of course, there was no glass, but reaching inside, he tried to see if there was anything anchoring the house down. Instead, he felt a dampness on his fingertips.

'Jim,' he said, 'something in here.'

Jim looked across from the vehicle and raised a hand up to his ear. He clearly couldn't have heard.

'I said, there's something in here, Jim.'

Davey reached, grabbed what was damp and pulled it out of the house. It was a handkerchief, and it certainly looked worn with age. There was mildew on it and instantly Davy dropped it on the ground.

As it hit the ground, something rolled out of it in one direction and something else went the other way. *What's that?* thought Davy. But at this time Jim was wandering over.

'What did you say, Davy?'

'I said there was something in here, look.'

Jim stared down. 'It's a pair of dice,' he said.

'A pair of dice?' said Davy. 'You mean like you get with Monopoly or something like that?'

'Well, a pair of dice you'd get in any game,' said Jim. 'Looks different, those dice, though, don't they? A bit more primitive. Wonder how long they've been in there.'

'What do you mean, primitive?'

'They look almost like bone. Oh, they're bone colour. I mean, they won't be bone, will they?' said Jim.

'Of course not. Don't be daft. Anyway, it all stinks. Should probably just throw them away.'

Davy looked up and sighed. There was a man now, marching across the green. He was one of those officious-looking types. He had a short moustache. His hair was neat and looked like it'd been ironed on. And he was wearing a jumper that spoke of someone whose clothes were dictated by rule, as much of the rest of their life would be.

'What are you doing in there?' bellowed the man.

'I'm doing my work,' said Davy. 'Who might you be?'

'Charles. Charles Elstridge. And who are you?'

'Dave, this is Jim. We're here to do a bit of work.'

'Work for whom?'

'Council. We've been asked to remove this item here,' said Davy, pointing to the small house, 'and a few other minor obstructions.'

'Obstructions to what?'

'Drain channel being put in. As far as I understand it; I don't question it. I just get on with it,' said Dave.

'And what's that?' said Charles, pointing down at the dice.

'I don't know, but they came out of here. Just about put them in the bin, actually.' But then he saw Charles rear up all of a sudden. The man took a step backwards, and then seemed to wheeze.

'I wouldn't throw that out,' he said.

'No?' said Dave. 'Why not?'

'You see the initials on that handkerchief? Those are the same initials of a man who was murdered here over forty years ago. Probably longer, actually.'

'Are you sure?' asked Davey.

'Absolutely,' said the man. 'I can tell you right now. Martin Baird. It wasn't pleasant.'

'Okay,' said Davey. He looked over at Jim, who was looking back with an anxious face.

'What are we going to do, Davey?'

'You are going to go back there to the van and you're going to fill up two cups of coffee. I am going to get on the phone to the boss, and we're going to report this to the police. And then we're going to wait to see what they want done about it.'

'That's probably for the best,' said Charles. 'But maybe I should get on the phone from the landline.'

'I'll report this,' said Davey. 'It's important that my name is there. Means the boss sees I've taken positive action, not just sat around.'

'Heaven forbid,' said Jim, making his way back to the van and the coffee that awaited.

* * *

DCI Seoras Macleod was taking a moment to not appreciate the view from his office. He was tempted to go downstairs to Hope's office, the detective inspector he worked with. Hope's office used to be Seoras's, but having moved up to DCI, he'd moved a floor up. He regretted leaving behind the view he used to have, for it was one of the best in the station.

Now, the view was just . . . well, it wasn't. He also thought about going downstairs because Hope was on maternity leave and Macleod was covering the murder squad for her. This meant he had a legitimate reason to go down and use that office. However, he was still also covering the other two units he oversaw: the art squad with DCI Clarissa Urquhart and DCI Emmett Grump's cold case unit. It was a large team when all were combined. They'd just been through a very rough time, but things at the moment were quiet, ticking along.

Macleod was quite happy with this. With many years on the force, he knew you should take the best of the quiet times when they came. When you were on the murder squad, things only stayed good while nothing was being reported or happening. When it did, you always looked into things that were dark and usually bloody.

There was a knock on his door, and Tanya, his secretary, entered.

'Got a package for you. It's in one of those zippies.'

'One of those zippies?' asked Macleod.

'Came up from uniform. Got a note with it.'

Tanya put the note on his desk and left the package, too. She turned on her heel to leave, and then she stopped before turning back. 'Do you want coffee?' she asked.

'No,' said Macleod. He'd already had two today, and he'd rather wait for a third one. He never knew when he would get called up along into the senior echelons. Macleod thought that coffee was the only thing that saved him once there.

Macleod opened the zippy and looked inside, seeing a handkerchief and some dice. The dice were bone-coloured, slightly faded, and Macleod didn't recognise the markings on them. There weren't the usual dots from one to six. Instead, there were different symbols on them.

Macleod took out a pair of gloves and began examining the dice closer, before throwing them back inside the plastic bag. He stood up, exited, and made his way downstairs and along the corridor into a tiny room. There were two desks in that room. One was not occupied at the moment by Sabine Ferguson but her boss, DI Emmett Grump, was in the room. He looked up from behind his desk as Macleod walked in.

'Morning, Seoras,' said Emmett.

'Don't say it,' Macleod urged. 'You never say that word. As soon as you say that word, something happens.'

'But if something happens, you're always in here.'

'I need you to look at these,' said Macleod and put the plastic bag down in front of Emmett, who instantly became excited.

'Where did you get these?' asked Emmett.

'Found hidden away inside a miniature house. Out over at Mellon Udrigle. That's a small settlement out on the west side. I don't know where it is, exactly. I thought I'd let you take a look at them. You like that sort of thing, don't you? Dice, Monopoly.'

7

'I'm not going to talk about the M word, but yes, I do like that sort of thing.'

Macleod nodded and looked behind Emmett. There, on the wall was now a small shelf that never used to be there. There was a line of painted miniatures, the ones at the end not finished. Emmett caught Macleod looking at them.

'Helps me think—helps me concentrate. Some people like classical music. I like to paint models.'

'So tell me,' said Macleod, 'do you recognise these dice from anything?'

'I can tell you what the symbols are,' said Emmett. 'This is a pair of dice from a game, Majik Falls.'

'Magic what?' asked Macleod.

'Majik Falls. Accommodates five to six people.'

'Well, they were wrapped in a handkerchief. Stuffed into a tiny house out in the green in Mellon Udrigle. . . . Why would you have some dice stashed away?'

'I don't know,' said Emmett, 'although I recognise the markings, but I'm not one hundred per cent sure on the rest of it. What edition they came from. What year.'

'I want you to have a look at these dice. See if there's anything special about them. We'll get the handkerchief sent off for analysis.'

'Good idea,' said Emmett.

'So where is Sabine at the moment?'

As if on cue, a tall, slim, Northern-Irish woman walked in. She also had an Austrian look about her, and she smiled as the two officers looked at her.

'Done something wrong, have I?'

'Time to get your coat,' said Emmett. 'Do you recognise these?' He pointed down to the dice on the table.

'No idea,' she said.

'You probably won't have played the game,' said Emmett. 'But we are off to find somebody who knows about these things.'

'I'm not saying there's anything in it,' said Macleod. 'This could just be stuff left behind. But say these are important, even if it's just in someone's mind as opposed to monetary value.'

'Of course; can I ask whereabouts they were found and what they were tied into?'

'Well, it's gone on my desk,' said Macleod, 'so you have to know it was murder. But it was a long time ago, and I don't want to go down this route unless these are important. So find out what they are. If they're two a penny, it won't be worth pursuing.'

'I think they might be important, though,' said Emmett, 'but I'll clarify before I go any further.'

He stood up, reaching over for his coat. Sabine dropped a bag onto her desk and then spun on her heel.

'Time to go then,' she said. Emmett walked past, and the two of them headed down the corridor. Macleod stood there looking at the disappearing pair of officers about to turn down the stairs at the centre of the station. He wished he were going out to do this. But more so now than before. He'd have to stay and watch—stay and run things with a tactical hand. He wondered just what was going to come at him this time.

9

Chapter 02

'So, what are we off to?' asked Sabine, finishing the last of her coffee in the car.

'Going to a specialist collector in Aberdeen. So that's a good two-hour run out and back.'

'You can't just like pick up a phone, send them a photograph?'

'Well, don't tell upstairs, but probably. But if I want to ask, well, more pertinent questions,' said Emmett, 'I might need to watch his reaction. You don't always get to really understand what a person is saying over the phone. Have you ever found that?'

'I'm usually okay on the phone,' said Sabine. But she was different. Emmett read people. He was quiet. He sat back, assessing them. But every inflection was taken in. Sabine was a woman of action, although she did like to think she could understand people, too.

'At least you will not look out of place.'

'What do you mean?' asked Emmett.

'Come on.'

She pointed at the t-shirt he was wearing. There was some sort of creature with a couple of heads, claws, wings, and a blonde-haired woman in shiny armour. Sabine wasn't too sure if she'd selected the correct armour. For some reason, she'd neglected to protect her head and Sabine thought that knights usually had some sort of helmet on. Instead, this woman seemed to prefer her hair splayed out, swinging round in a motion that made it waft through the air like she was advertising conditioner.

'All right,' said Emmett.

'Can you tell me something?' asked Sabine suddenly.

Emmett looked up. 'What?'

'I've gone into all these games with you. We've been playing board games; we've been doing our role-playing games. And I'm loving it, Emmett. But explain one thing to me.' She could see that he was looking a little agitated, wondering what the question would be. And when she pointed at his t-shirt, again, he seemed to recoil.

'That's quite a modest one. All these female fighters, all these good-looking witches, all the sort of sexier females on these board games and that, why do they want to A), show off their hair so much. And B), well, not so much with this one, but plenty of the others, not fully protect themselves with their armour. They seem to, well . . . they seem to require plenty of skin to let the heat dissipate from their fighting.'

Looking at him, his face reddened slightly, but then he rallied.

'It's just what they wear. A lot of the lands where we play the games, they're warm, they're hot, they're . . .'

Sabine smirked. She liked to get him on the back foot sometimes. 'Is this why you talk to me about doing cosplay?' He reddened even more. But then he beamed at her.

'That's not appropriate talk,' he said. 'You shouldn't be bringing that up.'

'It's just I have thought about it,' said Sabine. 'Where's the biggest convention we could go to?'

Emmett suddenly looked back at her. A smile went across his face until he caught her looking straight at him. And he retreated again. She'd reeled him in properly there. Caught the fish on the hook.

'Drive!' he said. She laughed out loud as she focused on the road.

The journey over to Aberdeen was uneventful, and Sabine always found this road long. It wasn't a terrible road, but it had got busy, especially as you got closer to Aberdeen. And they had to drive right into the city centre.

Once she'd parked up, Emmett led her round several back streets before they spotted the rather unimaginatively titled 'Tony's Games Supplies'. There was just a door at the front with a small window. The window had a grill over it, but through it, Sabine could see some of the tiny figures, similar to what Emmett liked to paint. Beyond that, she couldn't see much, because the shop was dark. However, the door said it was open. Emmett pushed the door, and a bell rang, and Sabine followed him inside.

If ever there was an old-style shop, this was it. Sabine could imagine back in the day, sweets being stored up behind the counter, rows of household products here and there. The sort of shop that used to sell everything, the one that was on most corners. But where you would have had toothbrushes, toilet paper rolls, washing powder, and liquorice allsorts. There were also small boxes of figures.

There was a book section, but with hardback books, thin but large, well over A4 size. And each of them had a cover that made Emmett's t-shirt look positively modest. Similar style though, plenty of scantily clad people here and there, either performing magic or swinging swords. In fairness, some were even dressed as space marines, and you couldn't see any flesh on them at all.

'Be with you in a minute,' said a voice from the rear of the shop. Towards the far end of the shop, there was a small door, which was lying open. Through it, Sabine could just about make out some tables and some figures sitting on them. The one she saw looked like a dragon. It was in a state of being half-painted. And then a shambling figure came in.

The man must have been about forty-five and wore a T-shirt similar to Emmett's. However, the creature on the motif was winged, and the woman was a savage. The man looked up, saw Emmett and nodded, and then turned and stared at Sabine.

'Tony, this is Detective Sergeant Sabine Ferguson, my colleague.'

'Delighted to meet you,' said Tony, and Sabine got the feeling he actually meant it. Without looking at Emmett, he said, 'Are you here for personal reasons, or is there something else I can do to help? He doesn't normally mention the police words.'

'The police words?' asked Sabine.

'I'm never Detective Inspector Emmett Grump here,' said Emmett to her. 'I've introduced you as DS Ferguson, not Sabine.'

'I was hoping,' said Tony, 'that you would be a convert.'

'Oh, she's getting there,' said Emmett.

'Well, it's delightful to have you,' said Tony. 'Can I get you a drink or something?'

'We're here on work,' said Emmett. 'Sorry, but here.' He reached inside his jacket pocket, and then, keeping them in a Ziploc bag, he placed two dice on the table. Sabine saw Tony's jaw drop.

'Majik Falls,' he said.

'Exactly,' said Emmett. 'Majik Falls, but . . .'

'But I don't recognise the edition.'

'The edition?' queried Sabine.

'Majik Falls has been out for a long time now, one of the most successful games going,' said Tony. 'The mage's dice have been produced in several colours and formats.' Tony turned around, reached up onto the shelf behind, and pulled down a copy of Majik Falls. He opened the box.

'This is the sixth edition, but a special sixth edition. You'll see here that the mage's dice are green, but a see-through green. If you look into the middle, there's a snake inside each die. It's amazingly well done. It's . . .'

'I'd love to talk to you about it, Tony,' said Emmett, 'but I need to know about this pair of dice.'

'Of course,' said Tony. 'Sorry.'

He put the dice from the sixth edition back carefully and then placed the box back on the shelf. 'Am I okay to remove them from the bag?' he asked.

'You got a set of gloves?' asked Emmett.

Tony nodded, disappeared out into the rear of his shop. When he returned, his hands were inside the same sort of gloves that Sabine would have used to pick up evidence.

'Why have you got those?' asked Sabine.

'Because some items I get in here are very delicate and precious,' said Tony, 'although most of the world wouldn't know it.'

He opened the ziplock and took out the two dice, holding them up close in front of his face. He then gently put them down before pulling a pair of glasses out of a drawer and putting them on. Sabine could see they had a light on one side and also the lens in particular places was more focused. The man picked the dice up again and held them close to him.

'How many editions are out now?' asked Emmett.

'Technically, we're on the ninth edition. However, within that, there are several versions of versions of each edition. I think there's a total of thirty-eight, at least.'

'Thirty-eight different editions of the same game?' said Sabine.

'Oh yes, it's not that unusual. It has to be a very successful game, and Majik Falls is one of the most successful. The people who made it were a small band of gamers. Steve Dingle, Orla Jones, and several others who used to game together. And they came up with the concept. Got it out there, as far as I understand it.'

'So, done well for themselves,' said Sabine.

'These people are millionaires because of this game.' Tony looked up at her. 'It doesn't happen that often in the gaming community. Most people put a game out and maybe it was okay. You get your money back, you may even earn a bit more. Some companies last ten years plus. But to be successful enough to be like a rock star in this world of ours, well,' said Tony, 'it doesn't happen that often.'

'Can you find out where these are from?' asked Emmett.

'Come with me,' said Tony. He disappeared into the back room, and Emmett and Sabine followed. He was sat with a laptop in front of him but he pulled up a chair and told Sabine to sit down. Emmett stood behind, and Sabine almost laughed.

Emmett should have been the one there. He was the senior detective, but Tony clearly preferred Sabine sitting beside him. Not that he was too forward or leering. In some

15

ways, Tony reminded her of Emmett. Emmett was awkward sometimes around women, certainly awkward with those he really liked. At times, she found he was almost shy with her, almost embarrassed, and yet she knew he liked her. But they were working together. That was never a good thing if you took it any further.

'Right, let's have a look then.'

Sabine watched as the man's hands glided across the keyboard. Soon, there was die after die appearing on it, and Tony kept shaking his hand. 'I was wrong earlier. I think we've got, yeah, nearly fifty full editions. Well, I can't find this one,' he said.

Standing behind him, Emmett nodded. 'What's it made from? Most of the dice there, they're plastic, aren't they?'

'You get a few metal ones, but this is not there, no. This is different; this must be a very special edition. Look,' he turned to Emmett and showed him one marking on one face of the dice.

'Do you see that? It's like it's been carved in. In fact, the whole die has been carved. It's not exactly completely square.'

'Manufacturing defect?' proposed Sabine.

'This hasn't been manufactured.'

'Are you saying somebody made these at home?' asked Emmett.

'The die has been cut, well, been worn down. I think it might even be wood. It's had something applied to it. Is it a lacquer or something? Something to keep it at least half the way it should be. But look at the markings.'

'What am I looking at?' asked Sabine.

'Oh, I see,' said Emmett.

'Well, does somebody want to enlighten me?' asked Sabine.

Tony stood up, disappeared back into the shop and came back in. He placed down in front of Sabine what looked like several versions of the mage's dice from the Majik Falls game.

'Look at these. These are four sets of mage's dice, all from different editions. See the way the dice are? Perfectly symmetrical. These are manufactured. These are set up, and these are made by machine. Except for the one just before those that you brought me. They were handmade, but look at them. Do you notice any difference?'

'Well, they're the same size and shape.'

Tony moved the dice that Emmett had brought. He placed it beside the others. He gave the magnifying glass to Sabine. 'They are not manufactured. Look at the way it's cut. It's cut by eye. It's just off. It's not a perfect cube.'

'And the markings,' said Emmett. 'Look at the markings. Mages' dice all have to be the same. The thing about Majik Falls is every time a new edition comes out, the dice have to look the same. In other games, it happens; different editions have different marking but not Majik Falls. It's a fundamental of the game. The Mage's dice—in fact, all the dice in Majik Falls—are not allowed to be changed. They'll be consistent all the way through.'

'And this one here looks like it should be the same, but it's done slightly differently here and there. It's like somebody made an inferior copy,' said Tony.

'Or,' said Emmett, 'somebody had nothing to work from.'

'Can I keep them?' asked Tony.

'No,' said Emmett. 'Thank you for your help, but they're part of a case now. They're evidence.'

'If they come out of evidence, I'll happily pay for them.'

Emmett smiled. 'I'll keep that in mind.' As they went to leave the shop, Tony shouted over to Sabine.

'Here,' he said.

'What?' asked Sabine. The man was holding a T-shirt. When Sabine looked at it, she gave a grin. The woman on it was uncannily like her. She was dressed like an Oriental warrior, possibly some sort of ninja, and her hair was swinging round.

'It's a double I've got. I just thought when I saw you, you reminded me of her,' said Tony. He handed over the t-shirt and Sabine thanked him. When they were outside, walking back to the car, Emmett nudged her.

'What?'

'I think he likes you,' said Emmett.

'Why do you say that?'

'Because he gave you a t-shirt. He's a geek. We don't give you roses,' said Emmett. He grinned as he walked away, and Sabine stopped for a couple of steps before running after him. But as she did so she thought to herself, *He's not the only one to have bought me a t-shirt. You did, Emmett.*' She found herself grinning.

Chapter 03

'I think this is worth investigating,' said Emmett. He was sitting across the desk from Macleod in Seoras's office as he sat studying the older man. He knew something was up. Emmett could feel it. More than that, there was a thrill because, for once, it was an investigation that was moving into his world—the board game role-playing world—which was normally devoid of major cases.

Rarely did anything break that caused national attention. Rather, they played at stories that would have brought national attention. That was the point of it. It was roleplay; it was gaming; it was fun. It wasn't real life. But this would be. This would be a real-life investigation. And it would be tied into the world he loved so much. It would be true to say that Emmett was feeling butterflies in his stomach. A little excitement, hoping Macleod would go for it.

'And these dice you say were handmade.'

'Exactly.'

'So,' said Macleod, standing up from his chair and walking over to the window, 'there's no possibility that somebody just dropped these dice then.'

'I don't think so. I think these dice could have been made

beforehand. Majik Falls is a massive game. You probably don't know it, sir. You won't know the world it's in, but in my world, in the gaming world, it's as big as it gets.'

'But couldn't they just have been put there?' asked Macleod. 'Couldn't they have nothing to do with the case? We've got a decapitated man killed out in Mellon Udrigle.'

'It could be,' said Emmett. 'But that case has never been closed. That case was never solved. I'm the cold case unit. I need to at least to have a good scan of it. Take a look through all the evidence and see if there's anything more to be had from this. See if there's any more lines of attack to follow.'

'What do you feel, though?' asked Macleod.

'Feel? Well, I'm trying to present the evidence,' said Emmett.

'And you're doing a fine job of it,' said Macleod. 'But what do you feel?'

'I feel these are connected. I feel there's something here,' said Emmett. He wondered if Macleod was testing him. Was Macleod trying to see if Emmett was letting his love of gaming get in the way? Wanting to jump into this world?

'And you say there's no other dice like these two.'

'None,' said Emmett.

'Well then, come over here a minute.'

Emmett stood up, walked around Macleod's desk and stood beside him, looking out the window.

'Do you know what I really hate about this DCI job?' said Macleod.

'The notoriety, the fact you can't go places without occasionally getting recognised. That people come after us, like recently,' said Emmett.

'No,' said Macleod. 'None of that. What I really hate is the view from this window. Downstairs in Hope's office, my old office, the view was fantastic. You could stand there, looking out for hours, and just think. Here, it's just, it's rubbish. And also the press; if it's a busy case, they'll stand down there. They can photograph me looking out of my office. My office is my cocoon. It's where I work from; it's—'

'It's your man cave,' said Emmett. Macleod raised an eyebrow.

'I guess so,' he said. 'This cave's not the same. Make sure you have a cave.'

'In fairness, my cave's quite small,' said Emmett.

'Give it time. These things grow, then they get away from you.'

'Get away from you?'

'That's the rub of it,' said Macleod. 'You get taken away from the proper work. I have an instinct, I have a gut feel, but it's harder to use from up here. I moved out of being a DI because I was holding back those who were beneath me. I moved up to DCI. Should have been up here five years previous, maybe even earlier. Should have been DCI down in Glasgow. But no, I wanted to be out on the street. I wanted to be in the middle of all the action, I wanted to make a difference there. To do that, you have to use intuition, you have to have a nose for it. You have to find that thing that's wrong. That's why I'm asking you about this case. Do you have a feeling?'

'Yes,' said Emmett. 'It's not just the gaming that's—'

'If I thought you could be swayed like that, I wouldn't have put you in the position you're in. You're a detective inspector now. And yes, you're a weird one,' said Macleod. Emmett looked at him, and Macleod grinned. 'Weird ones make the best. Clarissa is weird. You're a weird one. I'm a weird one. Hope is too. In her own way, I guess.' He smiled for a bit and

Emmett wondered if he was supposed to leave.

'Look into this. Go deep. If you're not getting anywhere after a week, let it back to bed.'

'I will do, Seoras.' He turned to walk, but Macleod stopped him.

'Like I said, don't let them bump you up too early. Don't let them take you away from the floor. That's where it happens.'

Emmett made his way back down to the office and then tore off to find some files. When he came back into the small office, Sabine was sitting, pondering over some previous work.

'Put that all to one side,' said Emmett, and he placed a box on her desk.

'What did he say?'

'He said, we've got a week. This is it. This is everything. So let's get the board up. Let's get going,' said Emmett. He could feel the excitement bouncing within him. Something was up here. He knew it.

He pulled out the files, passed some to Sabine, and sat reading them. After an hour, Emmett stood by the whiteboard with a pen.

'So, what do we know? We know a family man of four, Martin Baird, was found decapitated on the green at Mellon Udrigle. He had been dead for at least eight hours before being found in the early hours. Wasn't from the area. He was from Inverness. According to the report, his family didn't know why he was there. There was never any connection made between Martin Baird and Mellon Udrigle.'

'The forensic report at the time says that he was decapitated from behind. You have to know what you're doing to do that, don't you?' said Sabine. 'I mean, it's a skill to decapitate someone. Usually, people have to hack at it.'

Emmett raised an eyebrow. 'And you know this because . . .'

'Because I work in the police. I have had no first-hand experience but I know in several cases where decapitation has happened, people have had to work at it, as they say. And this cut was very clean. So, you'd have to know what you were doing. We've got an address for the families,' said Sabine.

'We need to talk to them. But we also have two dice found years after the killing. Were they there at the time?'

'Well, according to your friend, they look old enough.'

'Well, they're made in an amateur fashion. They're hand-crafted. But everything's not quite the same as the dice in the game,' said Emmett.

'So they could be a copy,' said Sabine.

'Or they could be something that was then morphed into the mage dice in Majik Falls. We need to establish that,' said Emmett. 'I think that's key.'

'Just one thing though,' said Sabine. 'You've got a couple of dice. It's more likely to be a copy, isn't it? Because there's only two of them. It's not like there's a complete game hiding in there.'

'And why are they there?' asked Emmett. 'Why are they hidden in that little structure? I mean, nobody's found them for years. Nobody's—'

'We don't know when they were put there. We know roughly when they're made, but we have no evidence to say when they were put there,' said Sabine. 'It could have been three weeks ago. So the idea that they're a copy and just dumped makes sense. We have nothing at the moment to say Martin Baird and Majik Falls are linked; therefore, we can't say they were put there by him or a killer.'

'Does it say anything else in the reports about him?'

'Family man. Three kids. Very unusual. No one knows why he was out there. Wife was confused.'

'Mellon Udrigle. It's way out on the west side. You wouldn't be there by chance, would you?' said Emmett. 'You wouldn't arrive out there by chance?'

'They believe he was decapitated there. So it wasn't a case of being killed in Inverness and then taken out there,' said Sabine.

'But he may have been taken out there to be killed.'

'But why? Why would you kill him there? If it was some sort of trouble, money or that, and there're criminal gangs involved, why kill him out there? There's no record of a gang war going on. There's no record of him being used as an example to people. That kind of thing gets around, so to speak. Because if you make an example of someone, you make sure it's known. Therefore, those in the community know, and from the reports, nobody in the Inverness criminal fraternity knew anything about it.'

'So we're looking for a motive that possibly isn't criminal.'

'Except that they must have known they were going to kill him, or what, a wandering samurai warrior was just there and thought he'd have a go.'

Emmett stared at her. 'I take the point,' he said. 'So, we need to establish why he was there, what brought him there, who knew he was there, and why kill him with a sword like that.'

'And why decapitate him at all? Why kill him?'

'Exactly,' said Emmett. 'What do we know? Well, we know that we have this pair of dice. We do not know where they've come from. The handkerchief they were wrapped in had his initials on it. Therefore, we can assume that he brought the dice.'

'There's always the chance that it's a coincidence.'

'In the middle of a big city,' said Emmett, 'I might have bought that. There's a possibility. But this is Mellon Udrigle. Nobody is out there. No. We'll see what the handkerchief sample comes back with. See if there're any links from that to do further investigation. We can't find the home of the dice. They're not part of a manufacture process. Therefore, they're done individually, and we can't find the individual.

'The place to go is the family. We need to check what the family says again about Martin Baird, if there's been any change, and also check into their background. There must be something. You don't get killed like that for no reason. It's not random. You don't end up out there in the middle of the night wandering around. Why is he there? No, we need to look at the family. Well, let's get ready to go,' said Emmett.

'Just a moment,' said Sabine. She turned away to the corner, and knelt down behind the desk. When she came back up, Emmett noted that her t-shirt had changed colour. She turned and was wearing the one that Tony had given her.

'What do you think?'

'I told you what I think. I think he gave you that because he's trying to make moves. Be careful with people like that.'

'Indeed,' said Sabine. She knelt down behind the desk again, and then a quick change came back up with the T-shirt she'd been wearing before. 'I think this one's better,' she said. Emmett looked at it, and then he gave a grin.

'That's the one I bought you.'

'Yes,' said Sabine. 'I'd say thank you, but you've got to watch the people who give you stuff like this.'

She watched Emmett's face fall. Then she smiled and almost skipped out of the office. Emmett shook his head. She teased him a lot at the moment, but he was never sure what it all meant. He had a case to do, though. He grabbed his jacket.

Chapter 04

'It's on the Markham estate,' said Emmett. 'We put it in the sat-nav. It'll get us there.' Sabine watched as Emmett punched in the address, and waited for the instructions to be given. 'That's not the best end of town. It's pretty rough, isn't it?'

'From what I understand, there are some rough elements on it, but there's plenty of ordinary, decent people. Just not very well off,' said Sabine.

'Well, then,' said Emmett. 'Obviously things haven't gone that well for her.'

'Well, her husband was murdered.'

'And her name is . . .'

'Ellen. Ellen Baird,' said Sabine. It took about twenty minutes to find the home, which was a small flat. There were four flats in a very traditional Scottish style. Like a house equally divided. Ellen had one at the bottom.

Approaching the door, Emmett knocked on it, and then stood back. It was opened by an elderly woman, which matched up with what they knew, for she was in her eighties. Her hair was tied up at the back in a bun, and she wore a rather drab-looking cardigan.

'Mrs Baird, Mrs Ellen Baird?' asked Emmett.

'Yes. Who wants to know?'

Emmett took out his warrant card. 'I'm Detective Inspector Emmett Grump. This is Detective Sergeant Sabine Ferguson. We'd like to ask you some questions about your husband, Martin.'

'Martin?' said the woman, and Emmett could see the tears already forming. She was gripping the door more than she had before. So much so that Sabine stepped forward, ready to offer a hand.

'Maybe it's best if we talk about this inside,' said Sabine. 'Would it be okay to come in?' The woman said nothing but simply nodded, and Sabine took her by the arm, helping her inside. There was a small living room, and Sabine placed the woman in a chair by an electric fire. Emmett sat opposite her, allowing Sabine to take the sofa that was in the middle of the room.

'I'm sorry to bring this up,' said Emmett. 'It's just that we're re-looking into the case.'

'Why?' asked Ellen. 'It was so long ago; they found nothing. What do they know?'

'I'm not sure they know anything,' said Emmett.

'So why, why bring it all up? Why are you here?'

Sabine came out of her chair and took the woman's hand, holding it. 'It's just routine,' said Sabine. 'It's one of the things we have to do. We haven't got fresh evidence, but we have had something happen out where Martin died.'

'What? What's happened?'

'We found some items, and we found them in a handkerchief, a man's handkerchief. The sort that you wash,' said Emmett. He took a photograph out of his pocket and handed it to Ellen.

'Does that look like one of Martin's?'

She nodded. 'What was in it?' she asked.

Emmett took the dice in the Ziploc bag and held them up so Ellen could see them. He then walked over with them so she could get a closer look. 'Have you ever seen these before?' asked Emmett.

The woman looked bemused. 'Why are you showing me dice? What's that got to do with anything?'

'These were found wrapped up in his handkerchief.'

'Why?' asked Ellen.

'We're hoping you might know,' said Sabine.

The woman looked at her. 'I don't understand how . . . I've never seen these before. It's just . . . it's just . . .' She started to cry and Sabine stepped over again, taking her hand.

'It's okay, but we need you to tell us.'

'It . . . it makes little sense. It makes no bloody sense,' said Ellen, almost shouting at them.

'Was there anything beforehand that morning? The last morning you saw him? Was there any—'

Ellen shot a look at them. 'It was nothing. He was agitated that morning. He was agitated. I told them that, but he hadn't said there was any issue. There was nothing, nothing about it. The kids, Lisa, Gary, Alex, none of them, none of them said anything was wrong. And then he . . . why was he decapitated? Why, why take his head? Why?'

She burst into tears again. Sabine stroked the woman's hand gently while Emmett felt at a bit of a loss. *How do you keep going at a woman who's had this happen?*

'Maybe we can go on a different track,' said Sabine gently. 'Your kids, you mentioned. Where are they now?'

'Well, Lisa and Gary, they've got families now. They've got

on. It hit them hard at the time, but they've kept going. They've managed to get . . .'

'But you have another child,' said Emmett.

'Alex. Alex was my youngest. The boy has struggled. He's gone off the rails. It changed him. Alex didn't handle it.'

'Where is he now?' asked Emmett.

'I don't know. I don't know. He doesn't write to me anymore. The others might know. Lisa, Gary, they might know where he is. They were better at talking to him.'

'Went off the rails. You mean . . .?'

'Drink, drugs. We were so happy. You've got to understand that. We were happy. There was nothing happening. There was no other woman. No difficulties with money back then. Yes, I struggle now. I don't have much.'

'Was he closer to any of the kids, more than the others?' asked Sabine. 'Was Martin closer to any of the kids? Did he have a preference?'

'No, we don't do preferences in this household. We never did.'

'Was anybody involved in anything that would have swords as part of it?'

'No. No, no. I would have told them back then. Of course I would have.'

'Your kids, were they into gaming?' asked Emmett.

'What's gaming?' asked Ellen, looking confused.

'The inspector's asking about board games. Probably board games back in the day, but dressing up even. Costume play.'

'We had games. We had normal games, board games. I don't remember those dice. Don't remember seeing those dice in any of them.'

'Did you play any as a family?' asked Emmett.

'On and off.'

'Any of the kids more taken by board games than the others?'

'Not that I can remember. We just played at Christmas and other family times. It's long time ago. I struggle to keep the happy memories. Do you understand that?'

'Are you able to get me the addresses of your children?' asked Sabine. The woman nodded and stood up, disappearing out of the room. Sabine looked over at Emmett. 'She doesn't know much. She's very . . . upset. I don't think there's much more to be gained.'

'She said he was agitated when he went.'

'Maybe he's one of those older men. Back in the day when a man had his business and the wife had hers. It doesn't work that way anymore.'

'Possibly. She doesn't remember the dice though,' said Emmett. 'Not surprising though, is it? If somebody's made these, you're not necessarily going to have played with them.'

'I guess so,' said Sabine.

Ellen came back and handed a piece of paper over to Sabine. Unfolding it, she looked and saw three names. Lisa Cobb, with an address in Glasgow. Gary Baird, living in Newcastle, according to the address. And then there was just the word, Alex.

'Do you remember anything from around the time?' asked Emmett. 'Anybody looking to talk to your husband? Anybody?'

'Nothing,' said Ellen, almost exasperated. 'I told them all back then, and they came up with nothing. You have nothing. Nothing.'

'Not so far,' said Emmett. 'I think we've taken up too much of your time.' He thanked Ellen and then met Sabine outside the house.

'This seems like a regular family. She looks completely shocked. She doesn't seem to have any idea,' said Sabine. 'This isn't making any sense at the moment.'

'Mistaken identity? Did somebody get it wrong with him? Take out the wrong man?'

'But you have to get him out there,' said Sabine. 'There's no obvious reason for him to be going out there. It looks like he withheld it from his family.'

'Well, withheld it from his wife,' said Emmett. 'I think we find out what the kids know. See if we can get hold of Alex, too. If he's gone off the rails, it may be more to do with him.'

'You can't be sure of that,' said Sabine.

'No, but it's a line of inquiry, and that's all we have at the moment. We need to just keep pushing,' said Emmett.

'Here's a question,' said Sabine. 'Would she have noticed if her kids were really into gaming? I mean, back in those days, how much stuff would you have had? Would she even have known what it was?'

'How much did you know before I introduced you to the joys of the dice?' asked Emmett.

'Not a lot,' said Sabine. 'Not a lot at all. Guess it depends on what sort of parent you are, too.'

'This is where we lack, you and I,' said Emmett. 'We've no experience of family.'

'Well, what do you suggest we do about that?' asked Sabine. 'I think it's a bit much to start one.'

Emmett shot her a look. 'Is this teasing going to continue? You seem to be . . .'

Sabine shook her head. 'Sorry,' she said. 'It's just that . . .'

'I'm the DI here,' said Emmett.

'And you kind of jumped ahead of me. Maybe I'm just trying to keep you on my level. Sorry,' said Sabine.

Sabine and Emmett had worked together on the Arts team, but while they were of equal rank, Sabine had been seen as the senior officer because of her expert knowledge in the Arts world.

'It's fine,' said Emmett, 'really, it's fine. But we're going to need to get some stuff together if we're heading for Glasgow and then Newcastle. Tell you what else we can do—we could pop through Edinburgh as well.'

'Because?'

'Because that's where Samson Games is.'

'You can't just nip off and start going to gaming manufacturers for no reason,' said Sabine. 'Macleod won't like that.'

'Samson Games are the ones who currently produces the new editions of Majik Falls. In fact, they've been involved in it for a long time. I think we should talk to them, see if they know anything about the dice. Tony's an expert and he's an independent one. But maybe we need to see what the people who make today's editions know.'

'So we're off on tour?'

'We've only got a week to get our teeth into this and find something, then Macleod's going to pull the plug,' said Emmett. 'So let's go pick up our stuff and get going.'

Emmett placed some calls, and it was agreed that they would meet up with Lisa Cobb in Glasgow the next day. They left the office and travelled the four hours along the A9 to Glasgow, arriving in the city late at night. After parking up and then finding a hotel room, Sabine pondered the case as she lay in bed.

She reckoned she was coming at it from a different perspective than Emmett. She enjoyed gaming and that, but surely there was a more human element to what was going on. That was the thing. Emmett would look at the game, but she hoped he would see the human element beside it. At the end of the day, the dice were superfluous. The main reason they were involved in the case was not to find the history of the dice. It was to find out who killed Martin Baird and why.

She tried to think about their line of attack, the way in which they were following the case. But Emmett was right. Check out the family first. He was also checking out the gaming company. Cast the net wider if nothing comes from that.

She lay back in bed. Then realised she was still wearing her t-shirt, the one Emmett had bought her. She'd brought pyjamas with her, but she hadn't put them on, instead choosing to sleep in the t-shirt. As she lay there, she thought to herself she didn't know why she was wearing it. And then she told herself she was lying. Of course she knew, and she happily drifted off to sleep.

Chapter 05

Sabine found Emmett at breakfast the next morning. He was dressed in a jumper that had a couple of large dice on it, and Sabine wondered if it was appropriate given the current investigation. It wasn't unusual for Emmett to be dressed like this. Macleod encouraged them to wear what they wanted to be at ease. It was just that Emmett always looked different. Sabine thought she looked a lot snappier, albeit she wore blue jeans with a blue jacket on top.

'You sleep all right?' asked Sabine.

'Just wondering. Got that feeling again. I definitely think we're on the right track. I can't put down just why.'

'Well, that's not much use,' said Sabine. 'Anyway, we're booked in to see this woman at nine. Lisa Cobb. We're meeting her at her fitness business.'

'She's not one of that sort, is she?' asked Emmett.

'I don't know. She may never see the gym. She runs a business. You don't have to be involved in a business. Sometimes you can just be the person over the top, letting others manage.'

'I don't think that's true,' said Emmett. 'You have to have some sort of passion behind it.'

35

'Really? What about those people who produce toilet paper? You get passionate about that?' said Sabine.

Emmett chuckled. 'But seriously, you've got to have some sort of interest, don't you?'

Sabine raised her shoulders. It was another half an hour before they were heading through the Glasgow rush-hour traffic to pull up at Cobb Fitness. It was on a retail park in between shops, but it took up the same amount of space as a large store.

The door slid open, and they entered what could almost have doubled for the entrance to a retail store. They saw a large counter with a couple of appropriately looking fit young people behind it, all dressed in tracksuit tops and t-shirts.

'Hello. What are we off to today?' asked a bright young woman.

'We're not off anywhere. We're here to see Mrs Cobb,' announced Emmett, pulling out his warrant card. 'DI Emmett Grump. This is DS Sabine Ferguson.'

'Oh yes, yes, I'll just check she's ready for you. If you want to, take a seat over there. Feel free to help yourself to a bottle of water or an orange juice.'

Emmett was disappointed when he couldn't see any coffee in the waiting area but he took a seat anyway, along with Sabine. It was five minutes before a smartly dressed woman entered the foyer. She was wearing a neat skirt that stopped just above the knees. Sabine would have put her in her fifties.

She carried a style. Her blonde hair, probably shorter than when she was younger, seemed to almost hold off her head. Lacquered is what Sabine's mother would have called it but nowadays, was it a bit of fixative hold? Sabine never used any. Brushing hers was enough to do.

'Hello, officers. My name's Lisa Cobb. I run Cobb Fitness. Please, please come with me through to the offices. Gillian, I'll be out of commission for half an hour or so. Just take my calls. I'll call everyone back.'

Sabine followed Emmett through into a rather smart office. To one side was a large computer screen, and several awards were on the wall. 'Gym of the Year' was plastered here and there, and Sabine could see photographs of Lisa Cobb with various celebrities who had handed out the awards.

'Now then, Detective Inspector, I think they said to me.'

'DI Grump, ma'am,' said Emmett.

'Please, call me Lisa. What should I call you?'

'Inspector's fine, this is the sergeant,' said Emmett. Sabine watched as the woman kept eyes on Emmett and only occasionally glanced towards Sabine.

'Sorry to bother you. We're here to talk about your father and his unfortunate death.'

'That was a long time ago,' said Lisa. 'Of course, I've never forgotten the whole incident, but we've moved on. I've got a family. The kids are all growing up now. I've got my business. I had a husband, but I got rid of him. Some men don't know what they've got, do they?'

'Well, that's true,' said Sabine, and saw Emmett cast her a wicked glance.

'We spoke to your mother,' said Emmett, 'asking about yourselves and whether any of you were into games. Board games and the like. Just to try to get a bit more of a handle on your family.'

'Well, what can I say? Gary's down in Newcastle with his family. He's doing okay for himself. Unfortunately, Alex took it badly. He has gone off the rails somewhat. He was never

37

close to Dad, but he was always struggling. Forever a bit of a loner. He was only twelve when it happened, and it shook him. Shook him badly.

'He was quite articulate, but then he grew very sullen and reserved after that. Mum couldn't handle him, and the two of them never saw eye to eye. Unfortunately, Alex has been off and on drugs and alcohol. In and out of different rehab centres. I helped him a lot in the early days, but I have my own family, my own problems and I've kind of lost contact now.'

'So you don't know where he is?' asked Sabine.

'No, but I do have a contact for his last girlfriend. Well, an address. I could give you that. Otherwise, I had a phone number, but I know it no longer works. Alex goes through mobile phones like he goes through pints. He's not the most reliable of people. Not at all.'

'You said he was quite sullen. Were you close to him? I know you've said you helped him.'

'That's more to do with being the eldest. Trying to look after the family to a point. There's only so much you can do. I helped Gary out too, but he's done fine.'

'Have you ever heard of the game Majik Falls?'

'The what? Is it on Netflix?'

'No, no, it's a board game. Well, a bit more involved than that. A lot of role-playing and sort of cross between Dungeons & Dragons and a board game.'

'No, not really into that sort of thing. I do fitness nowadays. It saved my life when my marriage was going down the tubes. That's why I got into it.'

Emmett shot a glance over at Sabine and she knew what he was doing. Yes, the woman had an interest in what she was doing. That's why it worked.

'Why do you ask?'

'There's recently been a find,' said Emmett, 'over in Mellon Udrigle, the place where your father met his untimely end.'

'A find,' said Lisa. 'I didn't read about that.'

'No. Well, we don't want any undue speculation, but there was a find of your father's handkerchief. It had his initials on it, and your mother has confirmed it was his.' Emmett displayed a photograph of the handkerchief on his mobile.

'I wouldn't really know,' said Lisa.

'Well, it also had in it these two dice, which is why I ask about the games.'

'Dice. Why was father carrying dice? Father didn't play games. Dad wasn't into that sort of stuff.'

'Was Alex?'

'Not that I'm aware of. You need to understand, my father was a quiet man, a civil servant. We didn't get involved in anything. We didn't get involved in causes; we just went through life. Put your head down, get your job done, come out the other side with your money, have your traditional family holidays. We were clothed; we were fed. He didn't look for more than that. Didn't look to be anything, you know? He was a family man, though. That's the way he worked. He was the one who kept the family together. A lot of time for us.'

'What about when you were younger? Did he sort any issues out for you?'

'More than Mum. Certainly, I mean, if you had a problem, you'd have gone to Dad. But there were no problems. We had a comfortable, if at times, rather dull, home life.'

'Dull?'

'Just in that there was never anything new, never anything we did that was just different, you know? Nothing out of the ordinary. Everybody always wants to talk about their life being exciting this, exciting that. My life didn't take off until after I got divorced. I followed my parents into a boring married life. And then suddenly, got rid of him. And everything's a lot better.'

'Got rid of him?' said Emmett.

'Oh, nothing sinister. I didn't bump him off or anything,' said Lisa. 'Divorce lawyer, though. In truth, he deserved it.'

'Why?' asked Sabine.

'Because he was playing away. No one in particular, but every now and again he'd be disappearing off with someone. I haven't time for that. I raised my kids, and I got out into the business world.'

'You seem to have done well,' said Sabine, pointing to the wall with the awards on it.

'We're doing okay. We've got some good young people. That's what you need. And you've got to look the part. Can you believe when I was running a home and looking after kids, I had five more stone on me. Look at me now. That's because I get time to myself, time to sort myself out, and don't have to run around looking after him, or indeed his kids.'

'His kids? Weren't they yours as well?' asked Sabine.

'No, can't have kids. Well, not my own. Kind of inherited his, came with him from his first marriage. That was the other mistake, going with someone who'd been married before and, well, I didn't realize at the time that she'd kicked him out. I wish I'd spoken to her. She could have offered me some advice, and I'd have had an easier few years of it.'

'So as far as I understand it, you don't know this game we've talked about. You do not know why, as I recall from reports, your father was over there?' asked Emmett.

'Well, I was in my late teens, and no, I didn't.'

'Your father wasn't playing around. He had nothing secret.'

'Like I said, he was dull.'

'Overly dull?' asked Sabine.

'What do you mean by that?'

'Overly dull people are the ones who can hide things,' said Sabine.

'Trust me, my father was hiding nothing,' said Lisa. 'Look, I wish we could find out more. I wish we could get the people who did this to him. But it's gone. I've left it there. It's in the past. It's where it's going to stay. I don't need closure. I just need to focus on myself and my business.'

'You didn't have any friends or anybody over in Mellon Udrigle?'

'No. No one. Ever. In fact, I'd never been out there. I don't think anybody from the family had been out there until it happened.'

'Did you have any friends with swords or anything like that? Or did your father know anyone with swords?'

'I wish he did. That would have been cool,' said Lisa. 'I'd have been one of the cool kids if he'd been running around with a sword or that. But no, he didn't. He didn't do anything. He was dull. Dad did numbers for the civil service. That's all.'

'You mean he was an accountant?'

'Not strictly. But he did that type of thing.'

'What about your mother? Did your mother do anything interesting?'

'Mum looked after us. Dad looked after her. When he died, well, we got through. I had to shoulder most of it. She got very bitter about that. She likes me for the kids I don't have, the kids that aren't mine. Fell out over that. But I keep in touch.

Like I said, I'm the oldest of my generation, so I have to look after her. I do my duty, but that's it. Dad always taught me that, to do my duty. If anybody was in trouble in the family, you go sort it out. He always thought that was important, but he never really had anybody to sort out.'

'Thanks for your time. We'll be talking to your brother as well, and hopefully, I can find Alex,' said Emmett. 'I don't know if we can bring anything new to light or not. If we find something, we will let you know.'

'Like I said, Inspector, it doesn't matter to me. You sure you won't stay for a coffee or something? Have a workout, in fact. I'm about to do one myself.'

'I have to get on,' said Emmett. He stood up and shook her hand, and Sabine watched as Lisa continued to stare at Emmett as he walked away. Sabine almost felt she was interrupting by forcing her hand forward to say thank you. Once outside, Emmett stopped beside the car.

'What do you think?'

'I think you've got an admirer there,' said Sabine.

'What?'

Sabine laughed. 'Oh, maybe she's like that with everybody. Lisa doesn't seem to be involved. She doesn't seem to be bothered. All very straightforward. Knows nothing about the board game. We move on to the next one. I think that's what we do.'

'Interesting about what she said,' said Emmett. 'Her father's taught her to look after those around. I wonder, was he the eldest in his family? He certainly would have been head of that family.'

'Indeed,' said Sabine. 'I don't know. I don't think she knows anything.'

'Well, then it's across to Edinburgh. Time to meet Samson Games.'

'You're looking forward to this one, though, aren't you?'

'Majik Falls is a legendary game,' said Emmett. 'We might actually meet some of the people who originally made it. And these people are worth a fortune. But more than that, they're worth their weight in gold for what they did. Some games they've produced since as well have been excellent. But Majik Falls is the big one.'

'So we're off for a little hero worship, then,' said Sabine climbing into the car. Emmett gave a grunt. He always took the bait.

Chapter 06

It had been a while since Emmett had been in Edinburgh. Prince's Street was as busy as ever. It was two streets back from that though where Samson Games had an office. These people had serious money, as seen by the number of employees there to greet those who entered the building and remove those they didn't want. Emmett felt he had to pull out his warrant card quickly because while they were a games company, he wasn't sure that his current attire looked sophisticated enough.

'DI Emmett Grump, Detective Sergeant Sabine Ferguson. We're here to meet Mr Dingle.'

'One moment, please.'

The pair were placed into what felt like a holding pen but were plied with coffee. It was half an hour later when someone came down to pick them up.

'Hello,' said Emmett, 'I'm DI Grump; this is DS Ferguson. We've been waiting a while.'

'My name's Sylvia Smith. I'm Mr Dingle's lawyer. I'll take you up to see him now. He's a very busy man.'

'Funnily enough, I am, too.'

'Well, quite, Inspector, I imagine you would be, but we're failing to understand why you're here.'

'It's in the course of an investigation. When we get up to see your client, we'll be able to furnish you with some more details.'

Smith barely looked thirty, but she seemed to be very sharp. While Sabine wouldn't have said she was unattractive, there was nothing particularly remarkable about her, except for her height. Dressed in the latest style, she wore a very snappy and definitely expensive skirt and suit jacket.

An elevator took them up to the top floor. They were led into an office that looked out over Edinburgh and whose walls had been replaced with glass. Emmett and Sabine were introduced to Steve Dingle, the owner of the company.

'I'm Steve Dingle. I hope you're fine. Apologies for the delay, but, well, we had a phone call to make. And Sylvia wanted to run over things with me for some reason.'

'Really,' said Emmett. 'You don't even know what I'm going to talk about yet.'

'That's why she's my lawyer. She knows these things. She knows what to do and how to say it. Anyway, welcome to Samson Games. Over here's one of our founders, Orla. Orla Jones.'

A diminutive woman stood up. She had auburn hair that she wore in bangs. Unlike the lawyer, she wore a T-shirt with one of those fabulous fighting women on it. She had large, round glasses, and if Sabine had to categorise her, she'd have said older geek, for she wasn't young. But then again, being one of the founders of the company, there was no way she could be. She must have been reaching her fifties.

'I doubt either of you has ever seen something like Samson Games and the experiences we produce,' said Orla. And then her eyes froze, looking at Emmett's jumper.

45

'Kronos Greek. You were at that. Were you actually at the event?'

'No, no, no. I got the jumper after,' said Emmett. 'From what I heard, it was quite something.'

'I was sad to have missed it. I wish we could have run the event like that.' She glanced over at Steve, who just gave a smile. 'I keep trying to tell Steve that we need to branch out into more events. Less of the marketing angle. Just getting people involved. We've made so much money already off the games.'

'Shall we sit down?' said Sylvia. 'Over here, I believe, Steve. That's where you want us?'

There was a table in the far corner of the office, close to the glass walls. Steve led the way before sitting down and then turning and offering everyone else a seat with his hands. Emmett sat at the far end of the table with Sabine beside him. Sylvia sat close to Steve with Orla somewhere in the middle.

'So, forgive me for being pushy,' said Sylvia, 'but I have other things to do. Why are you here?'

'Well,' said Emmett, 'the thing is that I found something rather unusual.'

He reached inside his jacket and, in the Ziploc bag, he took out the two mage dice that had been found at Mellon Udrigle.

'It's the mage class dice,' said Orla. 'Can I?' Sabine took out a pair of gloves and asked Orla to put them on before taking the dice out. She did so and then carefully held the dice up in front of her, bringing them in close. 'This is definitely the mage class. Where did you get these?' asked Orla. Sabine watched as Orla's face became intrigued.

'You've never seen them before?' asked Sabine.

'These have not been used as a version of Majik Falls. Never have dice like these been produced with the game.'

'Are they a copy?'

'There are slight differences,' said Orla, 'so I don't think it's a copy. They'd have to change something more than this. I mean, look at it. You would say it's the game. It's easily recognisable. If anyone was going to make a copy or a similar game, they'd have to change the symbology much more than this. Orla's hand was almost shaking as she held the dice.

'You sure we haven't made any like that,' said Steve.

'Can I just clarify that my clients have pointed out that these are not from the game?' said Sylvia.

'I got that,' said Emmett. 'I don't need clarification. I can hear them.'

'What are you asking them for then, Inspector?'

'I'm asking, "Have they ever seen these? Have they ever used them?"'

'I don't remember seeing these,' said Steve. And then he waved a hand in the air. 'Ah, coffee.'

A woman came in and placed down cups beside Emmett and Sabine. They were poured coffee along with Orla before the woman retired and then came back with a large double whiskey for Steve Dingle.

'The dice,' said Emmett, 'were found at Mellon Udrigle. I don't know if you've heard of it.' All three looked at him and shook their heads. He peered at them, but they seem to be telling the truth.

'They were actually found at the site of a murder. A Martin Baird? I don't know if you remember it.'

Orla let out a gasp. 'Yes,' she said. 'That murder was on TV. Well, the report of it was. We had a place out that way. Spent a lot of time there. You see, Mellon Udrigle, I don't quite remember that name. Although it's quite unusual, isn't it? I used to go on my summers up to Oak Bay. In fact, now I come to think of it,' said Orla. 'Mellon Udrigle? That sounds like . . . there was a funny name of a place up near Oak Bay, our place. Yes, that might have been it. I remember the murder. I think I was, what, seventeen? Do you remember it, Steve?'

'I can't say that I do,' said Steve, and then took a sip of his double whiskey.

'Just to clarify,' said Sylvia, 'Orla has said that she's heard of the murder on TV, nowhere else.'

'I got that,' said Emmett. 'I don't need clarification and if I do I'll ask for it. We found the dice wrapped up in a man's handkerchief with the initials of Martin Baird on it. His wife has identified it as such. This handkerchief was found only a few days ago.'

'But he was killed a long time ago. Yes?' asked Orla.

'Oh, well, around forty years ago now,' said Emmett, 'but nobody ever knew what he was doing there.'

'It was a particularly nasty murder, wasn't it?' said Orla. 'He was, well, battered or something.'

'Battered?' asked Sabine.

'Yes. There was something unusual.'

Sabine wondered if she was holding back in what she was trying to say.

'He was decapitated,' said Emmett. Orla nodded.

'What was he decapitated with?' asked Steve.

'I don't know,' said Orla. 'I can't remember if the report said.'

'Well, this is why we're investigating and what we're needing to look into. Did any of you know Mr Baird?'

'Why are you asking that?' said Sylvia.

'It's a straightforward question. We've got two dice that

are similar to those found in the game that has launched this company and made it what it is today. And they're in a handkerchief with Martin Baird's initials on it. I think it's reasonable that I ask the question, did they know him? I'm not accusing anybody of anything.'

Steve looked over at Sylvia, who gave a nod, and Steve then said, 'No, I didn't know him. Not at all.' Orla shook her head as well.

'This could lead to some bad publicity for the company,' said Sylvia. 'Are you going to be releasing the fact you've found these dice?'

'No,' said Emmett. 'There's not much point. They are a tool for me to find a killer. Once we find the killer, it might come out in evidence. But I'm not for putting it out for public consumption. Certainly, not at this time.'

'What were you doing in Oak Bay, and how often were you there?' asked Sabine.

'We would live there through parts of our summer, and that is partly how I got into gaming—those summers.'

'When you founded the company? There was yourself, Miss Jones; there was Mr Dingle here. Who else?' asked Emmett.

'Well, there was Jamie. He unfortunately died of a heart attack when he was thirty. And then there was Elsie. Elsie doesn't do much anymore, not with the company. She's earned her money, and she's off; she's not bothered.'

'Do you know where she is?' asked Sabine.

'Last heard of somewhere in Australia. She's quite the recluse, difficult to get hold of. I haven't really got much call to go looking for her. She's got her money, all good and fair. She's no longer in the business.'

'How did she leave?' asked Emmett.

'We made a fair assessment of what the company was worth at the time,' said Sylvia, 'and she agreed with it, signed the papers, and now the company's owned purely by Steve, Orla, and a few other shareholders. It's no longer just a private concern.'

'If you can think of anything or hear where these dice came from, could you get in touch, please?' asked Emmett.

'I will do,' said Steve. 'Absolutely. But, of course.'

'Is that everything?' asked Sylvia.

'For the moment,' said Emmett. He stood up and shook hands with Steve Dingle and then Orla Jones, before simply nodding towards Sylvia Smith, the lawyer.

Once outside, Sabine prompted Emmett to take a detour into a coffee shop. When she brought back a couple of lattes, she sat beside him and studied his face.

'What?' he asked.

'No longer Starstruck?'

'Bit different to what I expected. Orla, she looked like what I expected her to look like. But he was just a businessman really, coming in with a lawyer.'

'They had two police officers there. Lawyer's not a bad thing, especially when you earn that amount of money.'

'I suppose so, but it still seemed a bit much for an initial conversation.'

'Orla seemed interested in the dice,' said Sabine. 'Excited, don't you think?'

'I saw her hands tremble.'

'Yes,' said Sabine, 'trembled. And she used to be up near Oak Bay. Oak Bay, that's certainly close, even if it was sort of holiday thing. She spent time up there. Oak Bay is close enough to Mellon Udrigle.'

'And you wouldn't forget that name, would you? How could you forget a name like that if you were anywhere near close to it?' said Emmett.

'It was funny though,' said Sabine. 'When you talked to Tony, he told you that those dice were cut, made. They offered nothing. All they said was they haven't been in any of the versions, but they didn't say this is clearly a fake or this is clearly something made, handmade. They didn't offer a lot.'

'Maybe they were just prepped not to offer anything. That's what those lawyers do to you.'

'I hear you, Emmett, but I'm not sure that's the case. The more we get into this, the more things just don't feel right.'

'This is what I've been trying to tell you from the start. I've felt that way.'

'On to Newcastle then.'

'Absolutely,' said Emmett. 'If we make good time, we might even see Gary Baird today.' Together, the pair walked back to the car, ready to negotiate the Edinburgh traffic and head south.

Chapter 07

The car was silent as it trundled its way down to Newcastle, cruising along the A1 from Edinburgh, until Emmett's phone rang. He put it on loudspeaker so Sabine could hear as well.

'Inspector, it's Jona Nakamura. I got some results from the handkerchief analysis.'

'Jona, brilliant, hit me with it.'

'I got some DNA from Martin Baird's old clothing that he was found dead in. This DNA now matches with DNA on the handkerchief. We have, however, not found anyone else's. The samples we took from the dice before we gave it to you are coming up empty, almost like they'd been cleaned, except for Mr Baird's DNA.'

'So, it seems like the handkerchief was his, and he brought the dice.'

'I'm telling you what we found,' said Jona, 'not what it means. We have found nothing else from the site, but then again, there's been so many people over it, there's very little we could pick up that's meaningful.'

'Well, thank you for that, Jona. That's helpful. Speak soon.'

Emmett closed down the call, and he turned to look at Sabine, who was driving. 'So Martin Baird is there with the dice. The dice have got something to do with it. The game must have been part of it, or the copy of the game, whatever he was doing.'

'But we still haven't got a connection, an interest,' said Sabine. 'From what we're told, he's a family man. Why has he got these dice? And it's of a time when the game hasn't been invented, as far as I understand.'

'First edition was actually just before it. The ones that made the money would have been around the same time.'

'Serious money?' asked Sabine.

'No,' said Emmett. 'It was becoming a bit of a buzz around the place, but it's grown out of all proportion since then.'

'So we're saying that these dice were made, what . . .' asked Sabine.

'Well, they were certainly made before the game got mega money, but it was making money at the time. Decent, but not spectacular.'

'Nobody seemed to have an idea about the game; they didn't have Majik Falls in the Baird household.'

'Well, not that anybody's saying,' said Emmett.

'Why do you think they're lying?'

'I don't think the mother's lying. She came across very genuine, and to be honest, Lisa Cobb seemed to tell the truth. We'll see what Gary Baird says when we find him here in Newcastle, but really, I want to find the one that disappeared. Alex seems to be someone that nobody knows that much about. He was younger than the other two.'

'We're running out of track to follow, though, aren't we? We can't tie Martin Baird to the company that made the game. He's just a guy with handmade dice. And to kill somebody for that? Or was it something else? Why would you hide them there? Why?'

'Let's not speculate too much,' said Emmett. 'We don't want to get ahead of ourselves. You're right; we don't know enough yet.'

It was an hour later when they arrived at Newcastle, routing towards an estate just on the edge of the city. They found that Gary Baird was at work. His wife called him, and Emmett and Sabine agreed to meet him at his work. Taking the car, they drove to the Newcastle council offices, where Gary Baird made himself available.

'Mr Baird,' said Emmett, approaching him. He had to look up, because Gary Baird was tall. The man was dressed in a green shirt and tie, with jeans below. Civil service dress wasn't what it used to be when Emmett was a lot younger. The man had a firm handshake and a little smile.

'I'm not sure why you're here, but Lisa rang. Said you'd found something. Didn't tell me a lot. Said you'd say what was going on. There's the canteen in here that's okay to talk unless you need somewhere particularly private.'

'No,' said Emmett. 'That's fine. Anyway, I could do with a coffee and a sit down. It's been a long drive down from Edinburgh.'

'Edinburgh? Lisa said you'd come down from Inverness.'

'Inverness was where we started,' said Sabine.

A few minutes later, they were sitting in the corner of the cafeteria, coffees in front of them, and Gary was looking rather bemused, awaiting their questions.

'We'd like to talk about the death of your father.'

'Worked hard to get past that,' said Gary. 'Obviously it was an enormous shock to everyone.'

'I believe Alex didn't cope with it very well.'

'None of us coped with it well. When it happened, Mum kind of fell apart. Lisa took charge, helped me through a lot of it, and was probably responsible for getting me on track. But since then, I've got married. We're now a family of four. And yeah, I'm fairly happy. Can't say I'm lacking for anything. My family's good. I see Lisa every once in a while.'

'What about your brother, Alex?' asked Emmett. 'Do you ever speak to him?'

'Alex was the one who didn't cope. He just went off the rails. Drugs. Drink. He never really seemed to come to terms with it. Oh, I don't talk to him enough. I assume that's what sparked it but don't know whether it's still what drives him there. That's the trouble with junkies, isn't it? Once they get started, they continue. And the initial problems aren't what's causing it in the now for some of them.'

'Do you ever try to help him?' asked Sabine.

'If I'm honest, I didn't. I never did at the start, and I've now lost contact with him completely. Lisa was the one who helped. Lisa has a mother mentality. I think she's the mother hen of the family. And she does it well, because our own mother fell apart. I don't see her that much either. I write to her, phone her occasionally. She never got back on her feet. Never going to get past it, I think.'

'Your father was, forgive me saying, decapitated. Did you ever have any reason to know why? Was there anyone who had knife or sword play that hung around him?' asked Emmett.

'I said it all at the time to your people. No idea what he was doing there. No idea why he'd gone out there. It wasn't him. He was, well, he was pretty much like myself. I've got my job, got the kids. You drive the kids about. You help them do what they need to do. try to be a good family man. Have little beyond that myself. I'm not looking to change the world. I'm extremely happy with my wife. We're happy together. We're not extravagant and get by. There's holidays, you know, good things.'

'But Alex went off the rails,' said Sabine. 'Why? Why didn't he cope? What was he like then?'

'It was a brutal thing to take, but Alex was always strange,' said Gary. He looked away this time, as if he were dragging back memories. 'You see, he went around with older kids. They must have been six, seven years older. They were older than me. I was about three years older than Alex. Lisa's older than me. They were probably closer to Lisa's age, in fact. Not that she knew any of them.'

'Did you know any of them? Do you know who they were?' asked Sabine.

'No. I was too busy with my own things. Alex and I weren't close. He was a pain of a little brother, in fact. I remember though. Yes. Yes, I do remember. There was a girl. She had auburn-type hair. The one that looks like maple leaves. That sort of colour. She was nice, really nice. I remember it because I was a fourteen-year-old boy and I'm looking at her thinking, *Wow*. And Alex is talking to her. And all I can think is, how on earth does he get to talk to her? He's six years younger than her, at least, if not more. She must have been about eighteen. But I never knew her name. Saw her a few times with him.'

'What was your brother doing with her?'

'It was usually when I was trying to grab him to get him home or find him. So he was talking, just standing about. Never knew what they actually did. He disappeared. It was a different time then. You didn't track your kids. They went out of the house and didn't come back until it was time to feed.

You sent one of the other kids to go get them. That's what life was then. Not like nowadays, where you've got your phone. You can track where they are, where they're going. You pick them up, you drop them off. Everybody's vetted everywhere. Back then . . . it was different. We just went along with it.'

'Do you remember any of the other friends at the time?'

'Ah, there were boys and another girl or two. I just remember her. I think that's one of the things, isn't it? You're going through that stage as a boy. Suddenly you notice the opposite sex. I noticed her. That's why she stuck in my mind.'

'Have you ever heard of a game called Majik Falls?' said Emmett.

'No,' said Gary.

'Did any of your family ever play games?'

'We played board games.'

'You had Monopoly?' Asked Emmett

'We didn't play that often.'

'Did Lisa or Alex like board games?' asked Sabine

'Alex hated Monopoly. Really loathed it. Just wasn't for him, I guess.'

'Did your dad ever wrap things up in a handkerchief? Was it something he did?' asked Sabine.

'I don't remember him doing that at all. No, that's not something that comes to mind. He had his own handkerchiefs. They were a Christmas present, I think. Quite classy in those days, that was,' laughed Gary. Sabine watched him as he seemed to stare off again into the distance.

'Are you remembering something else?' asked Sabine.

'Just the girl again,' Gary chuckled. 'It's funny that, I haven't thought about her in years. You just brought back a, well, a nice memory. Never knew her name, yet her image is still in my head. It's funny, that, isn't it?'

'Sometimes things stick,' said Emmett. 'Was your family ever threatened? Did anyone, did you, ever see anyone contacting your dad in a nasty way?'

'My father was Mr Convivial. He helped everyone out; he sorted problems. Even when he went to deal with people who wronged him—and there weren't that many—he was there to be conciliatory. He wasn't a man of violence; he wasn't a man who got angry.'

'Was he wise, though?' asked Sabine. 'Could he handle himself?'

'I was fourteen. My dad was still somebody who could take on the world, though as a teenager, he was becoming an idiot in the way that your mind works as a teenager. Dad was just someone who dealt with the problems of life, matter-of-factly, got on with it.'

'Did he ever tell your mother about problems? Did he ever share with anyone in the family?' asked Emmett.

'He certainly wouldn't have told my mother. She'd have freaked out. She'd have lost it. That's probably where Alex gets it from. And me a bit, too. Lisa's more like Dad—very steady. Takes charge; sorts it out. Not overbearingly, but just in a matter-of-fact way. Needs done.'

Emmett thanked Gary Baird for his time and then walked out to the car, where Sabine got in as well.

'What are you thinking?' asked Sabine.

'I'm thinking that Mr Baird, our deceased man, held a lot of things close to his chest. Doesn't tell the family. It's going to be hard to find things out about him. I went through the case files. There was nothing picked up. No monitoring situation, nothing like that. This seems crazy. Suddenly decapitated.

I can understand why a lot of them went into shock and struggled to deal with it.'

'But we haven't spoken to Alex yet. We haven't got Alex's take. He's the one who couldn't deal with it, so maybe . . .' said Sabine.

'Yes,' said Emmett. 'Maybe he's the one who's the cause of it but hasn't been able to tell anyone. Has to hold it inside. Who knows? We need to find him.'

'Well, we got the address of that girlfriend.'

'That's what we do,' said Emmett. 'Birmingham. This trip seems to get longer and longer. I think Macleod's going to have a fit over the expenses the way we're going. He gave me a week to solve this. And so far in a week, we seem to be travelling the length and breadth of the UK.'

Sabine laughed. 'We've got to check it out. If we go down here and we can't find any other leads, who knows where we go? He's a junkie. He could be dead somewhere.'

'Well, we head to Birmingham then. Do you know where-abouts the address is in Birmingham?' asked Emmett.

'I don't know Birmingham well,' said Sabine. 'But if we head off now, we can probably get there in the morning.'

'Then that's what we do.'

Sabine nodded, started the car and headed out of the Newcastle Council offices. She cut across country to pick up the M6 heading down towards Birmingham. It would be a fair drive down, and they would need to pick up accommodation on the way. As they drove, Sabine could see that Emmett was somewhat agitated.

'What's up with you?'

'I thought this would be a dream job, this one. I'm still bothered by having gone to see Samson Games. They just, well, the lawyer. It's just not what I expected. The gaming community, we're more . . .'

'You're not talking about the gaming community, Emmett. Normally when you say that, you're talking about people who don't earn money out of it. Or if they do, they're really grateful to people because they're on the breadline about making their business work. At least that's what I've seen since I joined you in it,' said Sabine.

'I know,' said Emmett, 'but Samson Games. I mean they've made their living out of all these people. They've . . .'

'Money distances you, though doesn't it? Money can change you from your passion. It's a business now, just bringing them other things, things they want.'

'But a lawyer, a lawyer in the room. We were talking about the start of something. Talking about—'

'We were in there as police officers,' said Sabine. 'Of course, they'd got a lawyer in with them.'

'I suppose so,' said Emmett. 'It's just, there's a point . . .'

Sabine reached over with her hand, taking hold of Emmett's and rubbing the back of it. He stared at her, but she couldn't fix her gaze on him, turning constantly back to the road to watch what she was doing. 'I don't think people realise just what the gaming scene means to you,' said Sabine.

'No,' said Emmett. 'I don't think anyone does.' And then he gave a cough. 'Maybe you.'

Chapter 08

Y ou ever been to Birmingham?' asked Sabine as she drove the next morning.

'Briefly,' said Emmett.

'Do you want to drive then? See if you know where you're going. It's like a blooming maze in here.'

'I got the bus,' said Emmett. 'I don't like to drive around places I don't know.'

'Well, what were you doing down here?' asked Sabine.

'There's a big games expo. Board games and stuff. It's in the National Exhibition Centre.'

'And what? What did you do with it?'

'It holds gaming tournaments. It's got people there selling you their wares. It started off small. You can join into games, you can join in competitions, but now it's massive, an absolutely massive thing. It's truly wonderful. You meet lots of people here, like-minded people.'

'Geeks, like board game geeks?'

'Yes,' said Emmett, 'people like me, people like you.'

'You're putting me down as a board game geek.'

'You're getting there,' said Emmett. 'You might not fit the stereotypical look.'

'What look's that?' asked Sabine.

'Squat, dumpy, glasses, you know. They always say you're unattractive, if you're a geek. Unless, of course, you're in the movies, where you suddenly take off your glasses, you shake your hair, and you're stunning looking.'

'I take it you're talking about women.'

'Well, that's what all the books say. But really, when you go along, there's all sorts of people. You don't fit the image yet, but you're getting there. You keep coming out to these games. Keep gaming with me and we'll get you there.'

'Maybe I'm just trying to please my boss.'

'I don't think you pander to people like that. No, you're going because you enjoy it.'

Maybe it's because I enjoy who I'm with,' thought Sabine to herself. Part of her wanted to say it out loud, part of her wanted to tell him that's why she went. And yes, she enjoyed the games, but she wasn't a natural at it. She wasn't a geek, so to speak, like Emmett.

Sabine didn't memorise what happened in all the games when they were produced. She didn't take it upon herself to find out which designer did this, which artist did that. And she didn't wear those T-shirts all the time. No, she wasn't like Emmett, but that didn't stop her.

She caught herself. *We have to keep it at flirting,* she thought. *If it gets beyond flirting, it's going to be difficult to work together.*

'You know where you're going then?' said Emmett.

'I'm just following the sat-nav. But no, I've never been somewhere like this before.'

The part of Birmingham they were in seemed to be very run down. It was like most of the shops had left. There was an odd street corner newsagent. Here and there were shops selling vapes. There were charity shops too. The housing was of poor quality, like with most cities. It was a place that immigrants found because the housing was cheaper. They could afford it.

Sabine took two more turns and then pulled up. 'That's it, down there,' she said. 'Best we walk past them first. Get a good look at the place.'

'Why?' asked Emmett.

'Look at the place. It might not be the best to go in as a police officer.'

'Because?' asked Emmett.

'Because some of these people will panic. People might be here illegally. We need to find someone, not cause a mass exodus of everyone running away. The good thing is, you don't look like a police officer.' Emmett stared at her. 'What?' said Sabine. 'You don't. Got another gaming t-shirt on today. Just a moment,' she said.

Sabine got out of the car. She delved into the boot and pulled out some clothing before jumping into the rear of the car. Emmett looked away as he saw her begin to change.

'Tell me when you're sorted,' he said.

'It's not like I'm taking everything off. I'm changing my top and my trousers for some leggings and a t-shirt. Look like I'm nobody.'

Emmett was still looking away until Sabine told him he could turn around. She put the clothes she'd removed into the boot of the car and then together they walked down the street. Sabine took her hair out of a ponytail, letting it flap about, trying her best not to look like a police officer.

They walked past the building a few times, noticing that there were some boarded windows. Satisfied, they approached it, going on to a crumbling step in front of the wooden door.

There was no doorbell, so Emmett thumped on it with his hand.

There was a bit of kerfuffle behind. A voice said, 'Stay there.' And then the door opened. A large man stood there, larger than any man Sabine had seen in the last couple of weeks. He was broad-shouldered, and muscles rippled down his arm. He also had a broken nose. His hair was cut short and there were a couple of tattoos on the side of his neck that Sabine realised were from far-right gangs.

'What the hell do you want?' blurted the man.

'We're looking for a friend of ours,' said Emmett. 'She's called Precious.'

'Precious? What the hell sort of name's Precious?'

'She had this as an address.'

'Nobody called Precious here.'

'Are you sure?' said Emmett. The man leaned forward.

'I told you there's no one called Precious here. Why don't you just . . . piss off.'

'That's strange because the address we were given is here. We are in the right place, aren't we?' Emmett moved to take a piece of paper out. He produced it in front of the man. Pointing at the address of the building, he asked, 'This is the place, isn't it? I've got the right place.'

'Are you hard of hearing? I said piss off. There's no Precious here.'

'I'm just asking if this is the right address.' The man lifted his hand and put it on Emmett's shoulder. Emmett could feel him squeezing tight.

'This is the polite version,' said the man. 'Piss off.'

Emmett reached down into his jean pocket, pulled out his warrant card flipping it open. 'And this is the polite version,' said Emmett. 'Detective Inspector Emmett Grump, Police Scotland. I need you to tell me if Precious Hammer lives here and kindly take your hands off me.'

'Don't give a damn who you are. I told you to piss off.'

Sabine could see the man squeezing Emmett's shoulder hard. His hand then came across, pushing into Emmett's chest trying to drive him backwards.

'You set the inspector down now,' said Sabine. 'You take your hands off him and you step back.'

'What are you going to do? Hit me with your nightstick. Humph, sending a pretty young woman like you out to me.'

Sabine didn't like the 'pretty.' It made her sound like a doll. The 'young woman' she could forgive. She was reaching that age where when somebody said she was young, it made her happy. But she could see that Emmett was getting to a stage of pain he was not comfortable with. The man was clearly squeezing hard. She then watched him take his arm back, about to drive the palm of his hand into Emmett. She reached forward, grabbing the arm.

'Look, love, I'm not averse to hitting women either. Leave me alone and piss off.'

The man shrugged Sabine off and then drove his hand hard into the midriff of Emmett, causing him to stumble backwards onto his backside, the wind knocked out of him. He then turned, a fist swinging towards Sabine, but she was quick.

She stepped past that blow, grabbed the arm and yanked it hard, but the man wouldn't let his arm be taken up his back. He was stronger than that, and he swung his other fist towards her. But his stance was awkward, and there wasn't much power in the delivery. It caught Sabine on the shoulder.

For all that it wasn't as strong a punch as it could have been, she felt the impact on her shoulder. She let go of his arm, and he turned to come at her. Sabine ducked under his arms and drove an elbow up into the man's stomach. She followed it up with a couple of knees into the stomach, causing him to be winded. But he grabbed her by the neck, squeezing hard.

She had little time to react, and she drove her palm up into the man's neck, several times, causing him to choke. As he released her, she stepped back and kicked him hard in the stomach. He tumbled backwards inside the house and she followed in, jumping down on top of him, her knee following into the stomach as well. The man was truly winded, and she rolled him, taking out handcuffs, slapping them on his wrists. Behind her, she could hear Emmett. He was gasping, but was up on his feet.

'Is there a Precious Hammer in here?' he said roughly. There was no answer from the man on the floor.

'I'll watch him,' said Sabine. 'Go find her. Any trouble, come back to me.'

'Call for backup. Local police,' said Emmett, 'just in case anybody else comes back. Or maybe there's more in here.'

He left Sabine standing over the man and checking out her phone. As she made her call, Emmett walked through into an untidy kitchen. There were beer cans, bottles of whiskey and vodka sitting around. You could smell the cigarettes too. The front room had a TV and a sofa that was ripped to shreds. He took a step from it onto some stairs heading up to the floor above.

The first room he came to had a single bed, a sheet on it and various items around it. It looked like 'bedroom toys' as his mother would have put it. She didn't like to discuss things like that. There was another room, and he opened the door to see a figure huddled up on the bed in the far corner. He wasn't sure if the figure had any clothes on. It took him a moment to fully focus in the darkness.

It was a woman, very dark-skinned and shivering. Or was it shaking? Emmett stepped forward. The closer he got, the more he realised she was naked. He took off his jacket, reached forward and covered the woman from the shoulders. He reached down into his pocket to take out his warrant card, and held it up in front of the woman.

'Detective Inspector Emmett Grump. Police. You're safe. I won't hurt you.'

The woman looked back at him, but she said nothing. 'Are you Precious, Precious Hammer?'

The woman's eyes widened, although she said nothing, Emmett thought she must be her.

'I'm looking for Alex, Alex Baird.' Emmett sat down on the bed beside her, put out his hand, and touched her shoulder. 'Alex Baird,' he said. 'I need to talk to Alex Baird.'

'Alex,' said the woman. There were tears in her eyes. Her hair was a mess. Long black straggles running down her back. Emmett looked around the room for clothing, even for a cover. There was nothing. He stayed in the room with the woman until he could hear noise downstairs.

'That's the backup!' shouted Sabine from below. It was a few minutes later when she entered the room to see Emmett sitting beside the woman. As Sabine entered, the woman cowered away into the corner. But Emmett waved his hands.

'No, no. This is my friend, Sabine. Also police.'

'Who's this?' asked Sabine.

'She hasn't said. I've asked if she's Precious, but she hasn't said. She does seem to know the name Alex Baird, though.'

Once again, the woman's eyes flicked at Emmett when he said the word.

'Uniform's going to take care of him downstairs. There may be others to come back. There's too many alcohol drinks and the rest of it down there. He must have been just minding shop while the others were out. I take it this is why she's here.'

'Let's get the local services here. She needs to be helped. Taken in, clothed, fed. Somewhere secure. And then we'll talk to her,' said Emmett. He went to get up to leave but the woman reached forward, causing his jacket to fall off her. Regardless, she grabbed him pulling at his T-shirt. Sabine reached down, taking the jacket and offering it to the woman.

'Put it on,' she said. 'Put it on.'

The woman took the jacket, and Sabine stepped out of the room briefly. She shouted downstairs, asking that some blankets or some sort of cover be brought up. It was a few moments later, when a silver blanket used to protect against hypothermia was brought in. Emmett wrapped it around the woman, and she stood up.

'You come with me; we take you somewhere safe,' said Emmett.

'Precious,' said the woman. 'I'm Precious.'

'Yes,' said Emmett. 'I thought so. First, we take you and help you. Then you tell me about Alex.'

Chapter 09

Y ou're a long way from home,' said the older man across the table from Emmett. He was well built, but life had obviously paid him more than one visit. He was missing a hand, but still had the grace to smile as he spoke to Emmett.

'Just following leads up,' said Emmett. 'We ended up down here. Thank you for your assistance.'

'Well, not a problem. We didn't realize what was going on in there. Hadn't had any reports about it. Apparently, the place was being rented to Precious Hammer—the young woman you brought in.'

'Young,' said Emmett. 'I didn't think she was that young.'

'Well, late twenties, maybe into her thirties.' The DCI, Jack Primrose, grabbed a cup of coffee with his one good hand. He slurped it when he drank, which Emmett did his best to ignore. In the office outside, Sabine was running through some details with one of the detective sergeants.

'So, you're telling me, from a cold case that started up in the Highlands, you've ended up down here in Birmingham. The death originated in a place called, what?'

'Mellon Udrigle.'

'It's not that you have lots of unusual names up there or anything,' chuckled the DCI. 'The medical staff are with Precious at the moment. We're moving her into secure accommodation. Probably best to interview her there. I understand you'll want to talk to her, and obviously, we do too. It's not a problem. I have advised that we shouldn't wear her out.

'From what I can gather, or rather, from what she told the liaison officer so far, she actually was paying rent in that place and still is. We'll look into the landlord. These guys turned up, moved in and have started using her. She's paying cash to the landlord because she shouldn't be here. She's an illegal immigrant. That being said, the woman's being used.

'The liaison officer said possibly three to four times a day, men visiting the house. Sad case, very sad. We'll get her help and all the rest of it, best we can, try to put the squeeze on this guy your colleague subdued. We haven't identified him yet. Does he affect your case at all? Do you need to know who he is?'

'I don't think so,' said Emmett. 'If you just send a copy of what you find out to me, but I don't think it's going to be that important. We're looking for an Alex Baird.'

'Alex likely to have done this to her?'

'She was Alex's girlfriend, last that Alex's sister knew. That's why we came to the address. His sister had no other contact for Alex, just simply the address of Precious Hammer.'

'Hammer's a made-up name,' said the DCI. 'Probably because she'd heard it. Cash in hand, renting though. Not sure where she was getting the cash from initially, and then she was being given the money to pay the rent. But these guys were watching her when she was handing it over. You've probably pulled her out of a particularly bad time in her life. I'm sure she'll be grateful. Shame. Real shame. Still, you did something good today.'

Emmett nodded. 'So when do you think we'll see her? She's probably the last link in my case. It's a cold case. I've got to find Alex to drive the case forward.'

'Why don't you try to speak to her in the morning? She's not going anywhere. The woman will be secure. She'll be well-fed then. Hopefully, she'll be a little less scared.'

'It's a good idea,' said Emmett.

'And I'll join you, if you don't mind,' said DCI Primrose. 'Not that I think you'll say anything wrong, I just want to be there in case she says something that helps us.'

'Be in the room? Or maybe watch it from outside?' suggested Emmett.

'Outside? You think I'll cramp your style?'

'No,' said Emmett. 'She's just had men visiting her three, four times a day. I have to be in there, but I'll take Sabine in with me. I was the one who saved her, so to speak, so maybe there's a bit of trust there, hopefully. Sabine's a woman, so that shouldn't be a problem, maybe. But you coming in and standing in the background or lingering around, you'll probably . . .'

'I get you,' said Primrose. 'Yes, I'll see if they've got one of those rooms with a window. I can listen to what you're saying.'

'You've got my number. Give me a message in the morning of where to go and we'll meet you there.'

Emmett stood up and shook Primrose's hand. He opened the door of the DCI's office which led to the outer office. Emmett started to receive a round of applause and looked a little embarrassed.

'I think you'll find it was my sergeant who took care of the nasty man at the front door,' said Emmett. But the applause kept going. He approached Sabine and told her they needed to get out of there before his ego took hold.

They spent the evening at a curry house, feeding themselves before getting a good night's sleep. Early in the morning, at nine o'clock the next morning, Emmett received a text with an address, and the pair made their way to the new residence of Precious Hammer.

It was an unimposing building in the middle of the city and, from the outside, looked like some sort of failed academic institution. On the inside, however, it was homely. While there were medical facilities, there was also an area for bedrooms and living spaces.

Emmett and Sabine were told to wait in an area, and five minutes later, were taken through to a room where Precious Hammer was sitting on the other side of a table. Beside her sat what looked like a female orderly.

When Emmett came in, Precious looked up at him and smiled. As he came to the table, she stood up, walked forward and flung her arms around him. Emmett stood not knowing what to do. She squeezed him tight, saying, 'Thank you.'

'It's okay,' said Emmett. 'Maybe we could sit?' Precious smiled and nodded her head before retaking her seat. Emmett sat down and saw Sabine beaming at him.

'The reason we came to your address,' said Emmett, 'was because of Alex Baird.' Emmett saw the woman's face suddenly become agitated.

'Not seen Alex,' she said.

'Not seen Alex since when?' asked Emmett.

'Few weeks. Few months. Time, difficult.'

It was clear the woman's first language was not English.

'Speak Mano,' said the woman. 'English, yes. I speak a bit English. We speak English in Liberia. But I got little education. Mano. Speak mainly Mano.'

'We can get a translator, but it would take a while,' said Emmett. 'But you said you hadn't seen Alex in weeks, months.'

The woman looked like she was shaking. But she looked up with rather hollow eyes towards Emmett. 'I cannot remember. I think three months because I pay three months' rent. Only time I leave when I pay rent.'

'When you didn't pay rent, you were in that room?'

The woman hung her head and then nodded slowly. 'So, every day,' started Emmett and the woman simply nodded. Sabine thought she heard Emmett swear under his breath. Her own gut was sinking at the realisation of what the woman had been put through. 'So three months since you saw Alex. Before the men came, was Alex about a lot?'

'Alex is friend. Alex do drugs. Alex drink, but Alex okay. Alex help. We were close but men chase Alex away. Alex could not handle men.'

'Where is Alex?' asked Sabine. The woman looked over at Sabine and then back to Emmett who nodded.

'Alex is somewhere. I don't know. Lost Alex.'

'Tell me about Alex. Tell me what you know. Tell me everything,' said Emmett.

'Alex was a good person. Alex good to me. But Alex had very little. Not much clothing. Not much of anything. Alex liked to drink. Alex liked drugs. Smoked. Alex got money sometimes. Sometimes from family. But long time since it stopped. Alex. Alex had pain,' said the woman. 'Pain inside. He carried photograph.'

'Of his family?' asked Emmett.

'He not say who. Not tell me. Embarrassed to show me. But it not modern photo? Yes. Photo from back in day. Photo from time ago. Real photo. Not mobile. No mobile phone photo. Bit blurred. Bit fuzzy.'

'Who was in the photo?' asked Emmett.

Precious looked a little upset, almost. 'It was a woman. Girl. White. Girl. Very pretty.'

'What age was she?'

'She had just become woman. Growing up, just reaching woman.'

Emmett nodded. 'What did she look like?'

'Shorts. Jeans. White. Hair that was not brown. More like, well, hair that was deep of the fire. Red in a fire. Yes?'

Emmett wasn't quite sure what that meant, but he nodded anyway. 'What did you and Alex do together?'

'Alex liked games. He had cards. He had other games he found from charity shop.'

'What sort of games? Do you know any of the names?' asked Emmett.

'Cat, cat skin.'

'Never heard of it,' said Sabine. The orderly beside Precious shook her head too, but Emmett's face was alight.

'What did the box look like? The cover, the art on the front?'

'It had man with animal clothing.'

'Cat Skin, launched 1995, I think,' said Emmett. 'It's not a bad game, difficult to find. You'd have to know what you were looking for, you'd have to . . .' He stopped, seeing that Sabine was looking at him.

'Are you saying he knew what this was?'

'Nobody would buy it otherwise. The cover didn't do it justice. The game inside was actually quite good. It never sold that well because they didn't produce the artwork properly,' said Emmett. Then he stopped, realising three women were looking at him. He turned back to Precious. 'You play games. Anything else you did?'

'He liked games. He loved games. Board games. Games with board. Some games with card. Yes,' said Precious.

'Did you ever go anywhere with him?' asked Emmett.

'Took me to big hall. Big hall near train station.'

'Birmingham train station?'

'Not city train station, big hall with train station.'

Emmett's face lit up. 'Lots of halls, hotels around it, lake to the side, car park, big car parks.'

Precious nodded. 'Yes, yes, and tables, lots of tables, lots of games, games, lots of people selling games, lots of . . .'

'That's the expo; he's taken her to the expo,' said Emmett.

'Yes, expo,' said Precious. 'Expo, it was called expo.'

'Board game expo,' said Emmett.

'Yes.'

'This changes things,' said Sabine.

'Yes, it does. It does indeed.' Emmett's face lit up. 'But you don't know where he is now?'

'No,' said Precious. 'Men came. Alex gone. Alex not strong enough like you.'

Emmett felt a little ashamed at that. He was getting praise for being strong while sitting beside him was Sabine, who had really dealt with the situation. He turned to look at her, but she wasn't annoyed. She was just smiling. She could see the breakthrough, too.

Chapter 10

'Is he on yet?' shouted Sabine across the room.

'No, he's not logged into the chat yet,' said Emmett. 'Why?'

'I'm eating,' said Sabine. 'I'm also brushing my hair.'

'You're brushing your hair because you're going on a conference call with Macleod.'

'I'm brushing my hair because I haven't had time to brush it. You wouldn't understand about hair,' said Sabine. 'You've got to feel right with it. It's got to be—'

'What do you mean? It's just your hair. I mean, your hair just sits there.'

'Your hair sits there. Mine takes a bit of work to get it to look like this. It's either that or you've got to tie it up.'

'You wear it up, most of the time at work anyway, tied up.'

'But that's in a ponytail. Ponytail, that's fine. Tie it up properly, it's different again. If I tie it up fully at the back, that means it's not been washed properly. It's not been—'

'And you say I'm complicated around my games. The hair sounds like a whole board game in itself.'

'Oh, my hair's nowhere near as complicated as your board games,' said Sabine. She laughed and continued to brush her hair. Emmett watched her from in front of his laptop. Macleod wasn't on, and there wasn't much else to do.

He was fascinated by the amount of attention she gave to her hair. His just sort of sat there. Yes, he gave it a brush in the morning; he made sure nothing stuck up, but he didn't really deal with his hair. It got cut once a month. It was in the calendar when to do it, and the person you went to didn't charge you a lot to do it. Not like these women's haircuts. A hundred pounds, some of them, or more. *It doesn't take a hundred pounds to get your hair cut*, he thought. *It's crazy*.

Sabine put her hairbrush down, walked across the room and sat down in the seat beside Emmett. He'd been sitting awkwardly, as he was in someone else's room. And although he knew Sabine well now, and they partook in gaming activities outside of work, he was still awkward, especially in her space. Although it was a hotel room, it was still her space.

'Lighten up,' she said. 'You'll be fine. You know what he's like. He's always coming up with something. He'll press you, roughly. He'll try to get out of you what you know, try to dig out of you more than that. But he's fine.'

'I'm always fair and fine,' said a voice from the laptop. There was a blank screen.

'Are you there?' asked Emmett.

'Of course I'm here, I'm right here,' said Macleod's voice. But again, the screen was blank.

'Have you allowed us to see you?' said Emmett.

'Allowed you to do what?' said Macleod.

'Have you allowed us to see the screen?'

'Hang on a minute.'

Emmett could hear a door closing and decided that Macleod must have left the room. He turned and whispered to Sabine,

'You have to be very careful with him. And things like that happen. He's there, but you don't know he's there because he hasn't bothered to put his screen on. Should have seen it though in the corner. Should have seen he joined.'

Sabine was laughing. 'What is it with you two? Well, he's got a lot of faith in you,' said Sabine. 'A lot of faith, but you never seem to be, well, even like him and Clarissa. The two of them get on, even though she rows with him. And as for Hope . . .'

'Hope's his blue-eyed girl. Well, she's not got blue eyes,' said Emmett suddenly. 'Hope's his prodigy. Hope's taken over the line of work. I'm different. I'm awkward. He doesn't know what to say to me.'

'What do you want him to do? Talk about your gaming? He's more interested in crime. He's more into solving crime, and that's what we're doing. That's what you've got to keep it with him. On topic.'

There was a sound of a door closing and then a voice said, 'Ross, can you sort this? Apparently, they can't see me. I can't see what I've done wrong.'

'You just click this button here,' said Ross, and suddenly Ross's face was on the screen. 'Hello,' he said. 'That should be fine now. I think everything else is set up correctly. I'll try to see if I can make it easier next time.'

'You don't have to say it like that,' said Macleod. 'I just missed the button.'

'It's in the written instructions,' said Ross.

'Is that the dummy list?' asked Sabine, and then she clumped her hand over her mouth.

'The what?'

'She means the special list, the assistance list, the list for—' stammered Ross.

'The list for what?' said Macleod. 'The computer illiterate, the technology numpty?'

'As I said, it's on the list,' said Ross. He was now going a bright red and backing away from the screen quickly. 'If there's nothing else, I'll just get back to the case.'

'There's nothing else,' said Macleod. 'Next time, maybe you should put a title on the list so people don't call it the wrong thing.'

'Very wise, sir,' said Ross. Macleod had turned around to the screen and in the background, Emmett could see Ross opening the door to leave the room and wipe his brow. He was shaking his head.

That was the thing with Sabine. She didn't care if she dropped somebody in it. These things in life didn't seem to matter. The way people worked with each other, she found funny. Other people got worked up by it. But Sabine just took it as part of life. Emmett didn't find it so easy.

'So, what do we know? What do we want to know?' asked Macleod.

'We know we're missing one Alex Baird. And we need to find him,' said Emmett. 'I believe he's key to this case now. Martin Baird was decapitated in Mellon Udrigle. Why was he decapitated? We don't know why he was there. What we do know is that he had a handkerchief with him at the time that contained two dice from a game called Majik Falls. Now Majik Falls became a best-selling game and has earned those who developed it millions. The connection between Martin Baird and that game are unknown. The dice in question, however, are hand-carved. They may predate the game.'

'Do we know that for certain?' asked Macleod.

'No,' said Sabine. 'They may be early, though. In fact, we

think they're early. They're not exact copies. They're hand-made, roughly done. Seem strange if they're not part of some sort of manufacturing or ideas process.'

'You went to visit the people that run this game—that make it, yes?' said Macleod.

'Yes, we did,' said Emmett. 'They were not aware of the rough dice.'

'And you went to see a guy who is an expert in all of this.'

'Yes, that's true. Once again, he doesn't recognise the dice from any version of the game,' said Emmett.

'Martin Baird's family,' said Macleod. 'Are they involved?'

'Don't see how,' said Sabine. 'His wife has kind of gone downhill since it happened. The daughter—she's done okay. Lisa Cobb got her own fitness business. Eldest son, Gary. Again, civil servant. Quite a dull life, but a happy enough one. Seems content, making his way, earning a living. The only one that went kind of off the rails was Alex, the younger son.'

'What age was he when his father died?' asked Macleod.

'Twelve. Young,' said Emmett. 'And he's been on drink, drugs, that sort of thing. Moved around, family lost touch with him. We then went to see a Precious Hammer.'

'A who?' asked Macleod.

'Precious Hammer. That was the black lady whom we found in captivity.'

'Weird name,' said Macleod.

'Well, the Precious bit isn't,' said Sabine. 'The Precious bit is her real name. Hammer, they believe, she took as a surname because she shouldn't be here. She's an illegal immigrant.'

'And she was the girlfriend of Alex Baird? Is that right?'

'He visited her for a while before she was incarcerated by the men who were running her as a slave prostitute,' said

Emmett with disgust. 'He would play board games with her. Apparently, he was a very strong board gamer.'

'That's true,' said Sabine. 'Very strong board gamer. She told us some games that he used to play, and Emmett's identified some of them as you'd have to be very much in the gaming genre to know them, to have played them.'

'So, he's one of your ones,' said Macleod.

'One of my ones?' said Emmett. 'I'm not sure that's the best way to put it.'

'He's a gamer,' said Macleod. 'Every time you say something these days, people are funny about the way they take it. He's a gamer, okay? He's like you.'

'Well, without the drugs and the drink,' said Sabine.

'Where does it get us? You said he's missing.'

'He is missing,' said Emmett, 'because he used to visit Precious, but then she got incarcerated by these heavy-handed men and he couldn't visit. So, she hasn't seen him.'

'No idea where he's gone?'

'No,' said Sabine. 'We don't. Alex being missing is a massive issue for us. We think he can provide the answers. Nobody else in the family seems to know, or at least, is not telling us why Martin Baird was there with dice. Alex now, being a gamer, well, that could say something.'

'It could say something. He was twelve at the time, yes?' asked Macleod.

'He was,' said Emmett.

'Is it an age when you would make your own dice? Is it an age when you would be involved in a game like that?' asked Macleod.

'Well, I admit it seems strange. If you were developing a game, they go to concepts and then they play test. And then they bring it back, and they'll test it to the public. They'll—'

'But you wouldn't do that if you were making it from scratch at home,' said Sabine.

'Wasn't a time when people did a lot of that,' said Emmett. 'Nowadays, you have all these sites where you can get things printed easy.'

'But it wasn't done easily,' said Macleod. 'It was done with dice which are hand carved. Did you get any reaction when you went to speak to the people who have made the millions from this game?'

'Majik Falls, sir. Samson Games. To be honest, we're a bit surprised they had a lawyer with them.'

'I wasn't that surprised,' said Sabine. 'It's a company. Of course, they're going to have a lawyer with them. They have to be careful. Like everyone. She was just vetting what they were saying. Making sure they didn't admit any liability for anything. But they said nothing to us. There was no sign of foul play or anything like that.'

'Any connection at all?' asked Macleod.

'One of the women, Orla Jones, was involved in the original development of the game; her parents had a house not that far from Mellon Udrigle. But there was no indication that she ever visited Mellon Udrigle,' said Emmett.

'Interesting,' said Macleod. 'So at the moment, you seem dead in the water. Without finding Alex, you've got no leverage. If he can tell you something, if he can reveal where these dice came from, or has some sort of way of connecting them to his father, well then, you've got leverage with which to work against Samson Games. But at the moment, we've no reason to know or suspect that these dice caused any problem. But why hide them?'

'I think we're going to look at this from this angle. That the dice were an inspiration for the game. Not afterwards,' said Emmett.

'Explain,' said Macleod.

'The man died. He was decapitated. So, it's some random lunatic. Unlikely. But then again, these dice are found in a handkerchief stuffed away to one side. Hidden away. Did that mean that Baird had to hide them in a hurry? If they were valuable, if they were worth something, even intellectually,' said Emmett, 'it makes sense that he hid them. But who then comes and kills him? Who has a sword? Or a knife? Who decapitates like that? A crazy way to kill someone.'

'Not if you are slight and slender. If you can wield a sword like that, and it's sharp enough, to decapitate someone is one of the quickest ways to make sure they're not coming back,' said Macleod.

'It would all be in the dark as well. The real deal going on wouldn't be revealed when it went wrong?' said Sabine. 'I mean, if you're meeting away from everyone like this, if he's then hiding the dice, is he hiding his collateral for later in case something happens to him? Has he become worried? The killer hasn't noticed he's got the dice. Either that or he's got a great sleight of hand to be able to—'

'This is all supposition,' said Macleod. 'I think you've done great work, the pair of you. But we need more. I have got nothing to go on here. And I think we need to talk to Alex. You're spot on with that. I just don't see how you're going to find him. Precious doesn't know where he is. Where do you go? The family don't know where he is.'

'I might know where he is, though,' said Emmett.

'How do you mean?' asked Macleod.

83

'Expo,' said Emmett. 'The Board Game Expo is coming up here in Birmingham. He's not far from it. If he's still in Birmingham, he'd go.'

'Why?' asked Macleod.

'It's the board game expo,' said Emmett, looking in disbelief at the screen in front of him.

'Emmett, you say that like everybody should know what you're talking about,' said Sabine. 'I've only just heard of this, and to be honest, I don't think we've put out a good enough case to the DCI about why he should be there.'

'It's the expo. The expo? It's where all the new games come in. It's where you go round and you visit everyone. You can go and you can play competitions. It is a paradise for the gamer. It's massive. And he's taken Precious to it.'

'Emmett's right there,' said Sabine. 'It makes sense. If you're going to take someone to something important, if there's somebody you want to show—well, they're special—you take them to your important place. So yes, you might take them to the Expo.'

'It's a bit thin,' said Macleod, 'but on the other hand we don't have a lot to go on. Nothing really to go on. When is this Expo?'

'Two days,' said Emmett.

'Check if he's bought a ticket.'

'They don't really take down your name if you buy a ticket. You can also come in and buy one at the door,' said Emmett.

'So you've been?' asked Macleod.

'I don't tend to miss it. I was getting worried about this year.'

'You never mentioned it,' said Sabine.

'No,' said Emmett, 'I didn't.' The room went quiet for a moment before Macleod spoke up over the laptop.

'It's worth a punt,' said Macleod. 'Go to the expo. See if you can find him. Keep a low profile though. Don't want to be charging around. I don't want lots and lots of police at every door, every corner. See if you can spot him on the quiet. There's too many police, and if no one's there, we'll look a laughingstock.'

'We've had good help from DCI Jack Primrose. They're very happy with what we've done,' said Emmett. 'Pulled somebody away from a life of slavery. Life of—'

'Yes, he told me,' said Macleod, causing Emmett to sit back suddenly.

'I didn't realise you were talking to him, sir,' said Emmett.

'Called me up, wanted to know who you were, what you were doing. Told him you were under my instructions. Probably a half-truth in that.'

'Thank you,' said Emmett.

'Don't say thanks yet. Get down there. Get to the expo and see if you can find him. I think if we don't, this case is going nowhere. Get some sleep.' Macleod then reached forward before sitting back. He looked around. 'Well,' he said, 'it's a punt in the dark, but at least maybe they'll be able to do something. Looks like a bad case. Looks like a case we can't get to.'

'You're still on the link, sir,' said Emmett. Macleod turned and stared at the screen. He then started pressing buttons.

'No,' said Emmett. 'You've put your hand up, though.'

'Switch it off at your end,' said Macleod. Suddenly, he slammed his laptop closed, causing the screen to go dark on Emmett's own laptop.

'Maybe I'll phone him next time,' said Emmett. Beside him, Sabine was grinning broadly. And then she broke into her laugh.

Chapter 11

'Wow,' said Sabine. 'I mean, wow. And it hasn't even opened yet. Look at those crowds waiting to get in.'

Emmett and Sabine were standing at the National Exhibition Centre, or NEC in Birmingham. There were different halls within it. Vast halls. There to hold exhibition stands, tables, gaming areas. Everywhere Sabine looked, there was a stand with some sort of merchandise on it. There were tables with people there to demonstrate games. There was an entire area of just tables, side by side.

'That's the library up there,' said Emmett. 'If you go up there and you get a game, you leave I think it's ten pounds or something with them. You bring it out, you play it, you take it back, you get another one and you keep going. At the end, they give you your ten pounds back so you can try games, older games, whatever. Then in other halls you've got the bring and buy where people bring all their stuff and they sell it on for them. It's just busy as anything. It hasn't even got going yet.'

He looked around at the yellow-shirted volunteers. 'These people here,' he said, 'they're all volunteers. I've done it myself. Amazing, absolutely amazing.'

'What about security though? They don't do it, do they?' asked Sabine.

'No,' said Emmett. He looked around before marching over to a man in a shirt and tie. The man looked a little frazzled. He was talking to some other people in smart outfits.

'Could you be Mr Wiseman?'

'Yes I am. Who's asking?'

'I'm DI Emmett Grump,' said Emmett, producing his credentials. 'This is my colleague, Detective Sergeant Sabine Ferguson. Did DCI Primrose advise you of our coming?'

'He has indeed. Two constables are already up in the CCTV room. I can take you up there now if you want. We have got pictures put out to all my security guards. If anybody sees anything, they'll radio in. They'll obviously not intercept the man you're looking for.'

In preparation for today, Emmett had gone back to the family of Martin Baird and got the most recent photographs they could of Alex Baird. Jack Primrose, the DCI in Birmingham, had been a tremendous help. Already there were plainclothes constables at various places to help with the security. Emmett just hoped they could find Alex.

'If you follow me,' said Mr Wiseman, 'I'll take you up now.'

He marched across a corridor, opened up a door, locked it behind him, and then climbed up some steps. Turning round another corridor, he entered a room which contained several TV screens. Sitting there were four men in black plain clothes.

'These two are mine,' he said. 'Just here to help them. And those two are your constables.'

'DI Emmett Grump,' said Emmett. Two men jumped up.

'Constable Fraser and Constable Lewis. You can call us Jim and Frank.'

'Jim, Frank. Excellent.'

'You want one of our radios, I take it,' said Mr Wiseman. 'They're all on the same frequency. Obviously, you've got your own police radios as well, but I thought if everyone was in the loop here, it would be easier.'

'That's very sensible, sir. A good idea, Mr Wiseman. I plan to just be out and about. There was a roster of positions, I believe, for the constables.'

'That's right,' said Jim. 'They're all out there. We're all in contact. Good to go.'

'We open up in about ten minutes,' said Mr Wiseman. 'I've got you a ticket here and a lanyard. Just put that on and you can walk about freely. On the back of it there's a special card. If you need to go somewhere and people are stopping you, just show it. I didn't want to give you something that was so conspicuous but make you look like a normal visitor.'

'Excellent. I'll just drop our coats up here.' Emmett took his jacket off and was wearing a t-shirt with an enormous dragon on it. Sabine beside him was dressed in jeans and a t-shirt with a knight wielding a sword. 'We'll be out on the floor. You see anything, give us a shout, Jim. I'll let you coordinate the guys, let you do your breaks and all that. You all know each other. You get anything, shout it to me, though,' said Emmett.

As Mr Wiseman took them back down to the main hall of the exhibition, Emmett told Sabine it was probably best that the Birmingham lot were running themselves on this. After all, it was merely an identification mission. All they had to do was spot the man. At that point, they could hand over what to do to Emmett.

Ten minutes later, the hordes entered the hall. It took a while for everyone to filter through. Some were showing their tickets; others were picking up their pre-purchased ones from the stalls outside.

Emmett and Sabine wandered around. There were game makers from around the world, and Emmett pointed out to Sabine some of the newer games that were being displayed, along with some of the older ones. As they wandered, they saw a stall dedicated to Whirl Pit Games.

'That's the parent company of Samson Games,' said Emmett.

'The parent company?'

'Oh yes, Samson Games made a fortune. And the people in it, they sold it to others, but still operate as Samson Games underneath the umbrella company. They put special clauses in. So basically they took their brains, sold them off and said we'll produce for Whirl Pit Games by being Samson Games. But they kept all the royalties coming from Majik Falls. Very clever. They made an absolute fortune from it. Incredible contract they wrote.'

'You're quite in awe of them, aren't you?' said Sabine.

'I am. I'm also in awe of the game.'

Sabine looked over at the stall and she recognised Orla. It was hard to miss the auburn hair. She was smiling and talking to customers as they came along, demonstrating the game, pointing out other ones. It wasn't so much a stall like a market, but rather an area where they had gaming tables. Orla sat down at one to play a game with someone. Sabine went to go over, but Emmett grabbed her by the wrist.

'No,' he said. 'Let's not. Let's keep our distance. After all, that's not what we're here for. If we go over and talk to them and say we're here, after the way they spoke to us with a lawyer, I'm not sure they'll act normally. And I want them to act normally. I want to see if there's anything unusual. Not a forced effort, being on their best behaviour because we're here.'

'You're the boss,' said Sabine.

'Anyway,' said Emmett. 'Looks like she's going to be up on stage. Talking about Majik Falls.'

'Really?' said Sabine.

'That'll be interesting. Looking forward to that.'

The pair continued to wander around for the rest of the day and at approximately three o'clock in the afternoon, realised that Orla would soon be on stage. From an advantageous point, off to the side, they saw her take to the main stage. As she was introduced to the eager crowd, behind her on a screen played images of the game Majik Falls. The various versions of it and different people playing the game came into view. The five main classes of character who were in the game were represented behind Orla; the warrior, the mage, the assassin, the cleric and the bard.

'You'd look funny being a bard, wouldn't you? With all those others there. The others look really menacing.'

'That's the point though, isn't it?' said Emmett.

'What's the point? I've never played the game.'

'If you're the bard, you don't have great power, great weapons. But you've got the ability to lull people in. You've got the ability to communicate on a level that makes people dance to your tune, so to speak.'

'Really? Do many people win the game being a bard?'

'You have to play it right. I heard Orla put it in,' said Emmett. 'She was the one who came up with the bard but I'm not sure that's right. One of them was a warrior with a sword. Had a fascination for warriors. I can't remember if that was Jamie or one of the other ones.'

'You can't remember? Seriously? You remember everything about this stuff.'

'It was a bit more obscure, that. It doesn't really affect the game either. There'll be people here who could tell us, though, if you want to know. Anyway, she's going to speak. Let's see how she does.'

Orla's shock of auburn hair hung across her shoulders, and despite her years, she had a bright smile. She clearly engaged those out in front, who cheered before she even opened her mouth. She was wearing a pair of medieval boots, dressed up like a peasant lady, but she was grinning too. When the applause died down, she stepped up to the mic.

'Thank you. Thank you. Every time I come here, every time we get players in the crowd, it's just fabulous. I'm here today because Majik Falls is going to take another twist. We're going to do a space version of it.' There were gasps from the crowd. 'We never thought we could take the medieval world and put it out there. But I think we have. And I think it's what you guys want, yes?'

There were cheers, whoops, and hollers.

'I'm going to run you through some of the character names. Because we'll have five new classes. And for the first time, the dice will be different. Because the classes will. So you're getting five brand new sets of dice. And there'll be a space theme to them. They'll look like no dice you've ever seen before. They'll look like . . .'

She stopped. Emmett looked over. She was staring out into the crowd. He tried to see where she was looking but it was in amongst several people. It was just a sea of T-shirts and camera phones held up. Emmett grabbed his radio.

'Jim, where have we got the CCTV? Can we get the crowd

in front of the main stage at the moment?'

'Okay, can do.'

'Can you see anybody there? Is there anything?'

'Sweeping in. It's taking time. I can't focus on every single face. We're trying to sweep across. Do you think somebody's there?'

Orla was speaking again, but it was slow, and she seemed to refer down to notes or to some screen prompt, which she hadn't been doing previously. She glanced back up and out into the crowd, to the same spot.

'She's seeing someone. She's seeing someone,' said Sabine. Without waiting for Emmett to prompt her, Sabine tore off into the crowd. She tried to look like she was just a natural fan looking for a better vantage point rather than some police officer trying to shove their way through a crowd.

'We can't see anything,' said Jim. 'No identification. Can't see Alex. I can run it through later.'

'I'd rather we had it now,' said Emmett. 'We need to see if it's him.'

'I'm not seeing anyone. Should I send any of the boys in?'

'No, hold. Hold clear. Tell them to watch that crowd, especially when it disperses.'

'Will do,' said Jim.

Emmett could see Sabine now making her way through the crowd. Eventually she stopped looking around her, but Orla was back on full throttle now. She was no longer looking to see someone in the crowd. In fact, she was distinctly staring away from that patch.

Emmett could see Sabine spinning round and round. And then after fifteen minutes it was all over. Orla had finished what she was saying. She was back off the stage. The woman returned to her stand, and Emmett made sure the plainclothes constables were all around it.

But for the rest of the afternoon, they found nothing. There was nobody unusual. Nobody looked like Alex. Sabine headed up to the CCTV room and was still there when the doors were shut at six o'clock. At nine o'clock, Emmett brought her some food.

'Can you see anything? I mean, you've been poring over this for how long?'

'Somebody was there. You know it. I know it.'

'There's no face,' said Jim. The man looked weary. He'd been there since seven that morning.

'Why don't we call it a night, Jim? Mr Wiseman's still here, isn't he? He can lock up the place.'

'There's twenty-four-hour security. There'll be somebody for that,' said Jim. 'Back at seven in the morning.'

'If you can,' said Emmett. 'Tell the boys to stand down.'

And then, Sabine pointed to the screen. 'Wait. Jim, look. That guy there.'

'Which one?'

'The hood, the guy with his back to us,' said Jim.

'Leather jacket, hoodie, that's who she's looking at. Everybody else there is looking towards the stage; he's the only one who moves, and he moves when I come in, turns his back, but before that, we can't see him either. He knows where the cameras are. Either that or he's darn lucky.'

'In fairness with that hoodie,' said Emmett, 'it'd be hard to see his face from anywhere.'

'That's our man, that's our man, and he's back and watching Orla. He's there to watch Orla.'

'How do you mean?' asked Emmett. 'I mean, why does he

want to sit and watch this?'

'He's a gamer, isn't he?' said Jim. 'Maybe he wants to see about the new game. Maybe he—'

'No. No, no,' said Sabine. 'That's not somebody looking for the new game. You want to hear about the new game? Stand at the back of the hall and hear it. You don't have to be in the middle of that crowd. You can listen to that from a distance, or find out about it afterwards. He's there for a different reason. He's there to see her.'

'Really?' said Emmett.

Sabine looked over at him. 'You can come in here and you can take me to the cleaners about every single game in this place. How it's played, who plays it, how they do it. Which is the best version, what to get,' said Sabine. 'But see when it comes to people, especially people who have got something of a love or a crush for other people. Trust me. I understand that better than most. He can't be with her; he can't be close to her. He has to be incognito. The hoodie is not for us. Not to recognise him. The hoodie is for her not to recognise him.'

'I don't understand,' said Emmett.

'No, you don't. He has something for her. He's in love with her. Has been, long term. Something like that. Where does he know her from?'

'That's not necessarily Alex, though, is it?' said Emmett.

'It will be,' said Sabine. 'It will be. Trust me on that.'

Chapter 12

At seven o'clock the next morning, Sabine and Emmett entered the halls of the NEC in Birmingham. The place was already abuzz, but so far the doors weren't open for the expo. Jim and Frank, the constables who had operated the CCTV previously, were already at their station, and DCI Primrose was on the scene.

'They tell me you saw somebody yesterday. Did a runner though.'

'We couldn't get a facial ID on him,' said Emmett. 'Struggled to find him in the crowd. But he was looking directly at one of the women connected with the case. She seemed quite shocked to see him. I'm hoping he'll come back again today, thinking there might be some sort of tie-in.'

'Well, you've only got today and tomorrow,' said Primrose, 'and then it's over, I guess. What do you do if you don't find him by then?'

'If we don't find him? Well, then we're snookered. I'm not sure how far we can proceed with the case,' said Emmett. 'We've got a lot of loose threads, unfortunately, nothing to pull them with until we can find this guy.'

Primrose looked across at Sabine, and then at Emmett, and

then gave a little chuckle. 'You're certainly geared up for it, aren't you? I like the t-shirts. Where did you get them?'

'It's my T-shirt,' said Emmett, flatly. 'That's Sabine's.'

'You're into this stuff?' said Primrose.

'I'm a little bit of a novice,' said Sabine. 'Emmett here, he's the real deal.'

'Oh well, I guess it makes sense if you're investigating this world. Don't understand it myself. People with toys and models—why? What's the point of that? I thought you only had that when you were young.'

'Boys never lose their toys,' said Sabine, 'no matter what age they are. I'm sure you've got your own version.'

Primrose held up his hand. 'Well yes, I guess so. Good luck today.'

The hordes were in at nine o'clock once again, and Sabine stood near the entrance looking for anyone entering wearing a grey hoodie. She wondered just how brazen the man would be again. Would he get closer to Orla? Would he come again? Was it Alex? It must have been. And if it was Alex, why was Orla so shocked? Maybe it wasn't Alex. Maybe it was someone else. Who knew? There was only one way to find out, and that was to catch the man if he came back.

There were too many what-ifs, too many things that were uncertain to be sure that they were even chasing the right man. After the weekend, if nothing had come to light, then yes, they would have to head back north. Emmett couldn't see Macleod paying for this investigation beyond the weekend. Not when he knew nothing else. They'd have to dig from base, go through the computers, see if there was anything there. But he wasn't hopeful.

'I think I've got something,' said Jim's voice across the radio.

'Who and where?' asked Sabine.

'Somewhere by the gaming tables. Man with a grey hood. I think it's a man. Close to six feet. Can't get a good look at his face. By the fourth table, down from where the library is.'

Emmett and Sabine tore through the crowd, but then she tried to approach gently as she got closer. When they got near the area where the man had been seen, looking down the tables, she could see Jim was spot on. Four tables down, there was a grey hood, but there were a couple of people across from him. A game was out in front of them. Sabine approached and then sat down beside the man. The man opposite looked at her.

'You wanting to play? I mean, that's grand, but you could ask.'

'No, I'm just wanting to talk to this man here,' said Sabine. She reached inside her jeans, pulled out a warrant card, and put it down gently on the table. 'There's no need for alarm,' she said, but her eyes watched in case the man made a run for it. 'Can I ask for some ID and who you are?'

'My name's Mike. Mike Green.'

'Well, Mr Green, where do you come from?'

'I live on the south coast.'

'And what do you do for a living?'

'I'm a software engineer. Why? What do you need to know?'

'Have you got some formal ID on you?' asked Sabine.

The man reached inside his pocket, then took out his driving license, giving it to Sabine.

'What are you giving Mike this hassle for?' said one friend.

'You know Mike, do you?' asked Sabine.

'I've known Mike for twenty years.'

'And you're convinced that Mike's a software engineer working on the south coast?'

'Mike's always lived on the south coast. We were at school together.' The man delved into his own jacket and took out ID.

'Thank you. A case of mistaken identity,' said Sabine.

She looked around and saw Emmett standing nearby. She shook her head. It was bound to happen. After all, the grey hooded sweatshirt wasn't exactly unknown among gamers. Together they wandered through the different halls before Sabine once again spotted Orla. She was moving through the crowd, making her way to her stall. Once on it, Sabine watched from a distance.

'I think I'll wander round,' said Emmett, 'if you're going to perch here.'

'I think she's the key. Might not be a bad idea for you to be elsewhere, though. We can pincer in on him if he's here.'

'Very good,' said Emmett. 'I'll be in the next hall for a bit.'

He walked off and left Sabine standing at a stall with many tiny figures. She began glancing at them but then swept her eyes across the crowd that were at the Whirl Pit Games stall.

Orla was being her engaging self, smiling, and looked quite taken by the game she was playing. Sabine had been wondering if this would be a complete bust. After all, would he come back again? Why was he here? Why did he get a look at Orla? Why there? What did Alex's face mean, if indeed it was Alex?

They were running on supposition at the moment. They needed to get something firm. Macleod didn't like hunches. Well, that wasn't true. He didn't mind them as long as you backed them up, as long as you found something.

As she stood behind some miniatures, Sabine could see Orla's face. She had gone back into the main part of the stall and was serving a customer when suddenly her face seemed to fall. She looked momentarily sad, regretful, and then afraid.

Sabine's eyes roamed the crowd. There was a leather jacket with a hoodie under it. The hood was pulled tight around the head, but now Orla could see the face from the angle she was at; she could see the face.

Sabine moved quickly. She stepped this way and that, and was within ten feet, when suddenly someone bumped her.

'Oi!' said a voice. 'Take it easy.'

The grey hood looked momentarily in her direction, but not enough for Sabine to catch a proper look at the face. Instead, the man in the grey hood tore off in a different direction. Sabine kept her eyes on him as she grabbed her radio.

'All teams. I have him. We're in front of the Whirl Pit Games stall. Heading away from that, towards the second hall, towards the second hall. We're still in the middle of the first one, though. No, no, he's cutting back.'

Sabine began to run and then saw one of the plainclothes policemen coming from a different angle. Unfortunately, the man in the grey hood saw him too, turned and started running down another passage between stalls.

'Close off Hall One. Close off Hall One,' said Sabine. And then the man turned round a book stall, past one of the writers Sabine had seen the previous day. There was a narrow alley down between the stalls after that. When she turned in, she couldn't see him. She ran along it, cut out through another patch, and then she saw what the man had done. He must have spotted another grey hood, because now there were two.

'I've got two grey hoods, two grey hoods, near the food stall.'

'One's gone over towards Limelight Books. Limelight Books. Someone take that one. Who's got it?'

'Got them on CCTV,' said Jim. 'Trying to trail them both.

But there's a third now,' said Jim.

Sabine had eyes everywhere. She still had the two hoods in sight, but now there was another one. 'I'm taking the one heading towards the food court,' said Sabine.

'Tagged on Limelight Books,' said another voice.

'I've got the third on CCTV,' said Jim. 'Currently turning back, heading back into the main hall.'

'Have we got anybody on the doors yet? Get the doors,' said Emmett. 'Tell security. Full lockdown.' Sabine was having trouble keeping up with her own target. The man moved this way and that, and then he just seemed to vanish. There was a crowd of people, and then he was gone.

'Lost mine. Jim, have you seen him?'

'I've got five now,' said Jim.

'What do you mean you've got five?'

'Calm down,' said Emmett. 'We've got the doors. Put the main security on the doors. Nobody with a hood's getting out.'

'Go full lockdown,' said Sabine. 'Full lockdown. It's the only way. You can take hood off, just get out.'

'Calling it,' said Emmett.

Sabine ran round and round, but the area was so busy. It was hard to catch a face, hard to glimpse the grey hood. He could be anywhere by now.

'Got one at the doors,' came a voice.

'Got mine,' said another voice.

'Third one's being covered off. Where's four?' said Emmett. 'Jim, where's four? Where's the other one?'

'Other one's gone,' said Sabine. She ran towards the front entrance over to security stationed there. They shook their heads, but Sabine saw another man in the distance with a grey hood. Was this the one from before? She couldn't be sure.

This time she ran, narrowly avoiding people. She put a hand on the man's shoulder. He turned around. 'Yes?'

When he pulled the hood down, he was old. Maybe in his 60s. Too old.

'Can I ask your name, please?' said Sabine.

'Who's asking?'

'This way a second,' said Sabine. She took the man to one side and pulled out a warrant card. 'I'd just like a name, some ID, please.' The man produced some. A moment later, a woman ran up.

'What are you doing?' she said.

'This sergeant from the police wanted to speak to me.'

'What have you done, Michael?'

'He's done nothing. We were just looking for someone with similar clothes on,' said Sabine.

She turned away. There were no more figures. Nobody else to find. In another room, the three men with grey hoods were being talked to by Emmett and then being let go quickly. They weren't the right people.

* * *

It was eight o'clock that night, and the place had emptied. They had stood watching everyone leave throughout the day. They couldn't contain everyone for ever. Not when no crime had been committed.

Where had Alex gone, if indeed it was he? He'd been there, in the middle of the expo. Orla had noticed him. Sabine suggested to Emmett that they simply talk to Orla, but Emmett said no. He was worried that Orla might actually know him, might communicate with him.

Besides, what could they go at her with at the moment? She'd seen someone and looked shocked. The man hadn't actually approached her. The man hadn't laid a finger on her. She hadn't moved toward him. It was easy for her to bluff her way out. And she would know that they knew something about her.

Emmett wanted to let it run. They could always talk to her after the event. There was always tomorrow as well. They might come back.

Sabine and Emmett went to bed that night, frustrated. It felt like they were so close in the case. Alex was there, Sabine was sure of it, but he hadn't been captured. They hadn't got him.

Early next morning, they were back for the last day of the expo. At half past seven, they were once again setting up their CCTV and their routines to find Alex. This time, all his movements were going to be watched from a distance. As they sat, grabbing a last-minute coffee before the day would start fully, Emmett and Sabine were approached by an older woman in a large trench coat. She was making a direct path towards them.

'I'm looking for DI Emmett Grump,' said the woman. She pulled out a warrant card. 'It's DCI Travers.'

'I'm Grump,' said Emmett. 'How can I help you?'

'I believe you've been looking for someone in a grey hood the last couple of days,' said DCI Travers. She was an older woman, maybe in her sixties.

'That's right, here at the NEC. We were chasing him yesterday.'

'Well, I've found him,' said Travers. 'Or rather, the hotel just across from here found him.'

'Brilliant,' said Emmett. 'I'd like to talk to him.'

'Well, you better get one of them mediums. He's dead.'

Chapter 13

'**D**ead,' said Emmett. 'How?'

'Well, we haven't had a proper examination of the body, but by the looks of it, forensics said the neck was snapped.'

'Snapped,' said Sabine. 'Like from a fall or from . . .'

'Like somebody walked up behind him,' said Travers. 'Professional. Broke his neck. There and then.'

Sabine flashed a look at Emmett, but he was stony-faced.

'Can I see?' asked Emmett.

'I've got a few questions of my own,' said Travers. 'I want to know about this guy. I want to know what you're doing. This is now a murder inquiry, and this is my case.'

'His name,' began Emmett, but was interrupted.

'His name,' said DCI Travers, 'is Alex Baird. Found ID on him.'

'What sort of ID?'

'Well, looks like a bus pass.'

'Anything else?' asked Emmett.

'Nothing photographic. Library card, though.'

'Any credit cards on him?'

'No, he did not. Had a fair bit of cash on him. No phone,

though.'

'Not conclusive, then.'

'Well, no. Give us a moment,' said Travers. 'It's only just been reported. I've barely been here an hour. What happened yesterday?'

Sabine related the events, and how the different men with grey hoods had been apprehended. But she thought one had got away.

'So, this woman, who looks shocked, who's she?' asked Travers.

'Her name's Orla Jones. She's one of the founders of a game called Majik Falls. It's at the centre of our investigation. I'm looking into a previous unsolved murder of one Martin Baird.'

'Related to Alex?' asked Travers.

'Father. Decapitated.'

'Looks like the family's got a great sense of friends then.'

'Father died almost forty years ago. We think the game might be involved,' said Emmett.

'And this Orla Jones, what was she doing here?' asked Travers.

'She's in one of the stalls—Whirl Pit Games. It's the parent company of Samson Games. They were the people who originally produced Majik Falls.'

'But what happened with Alex and Orla?'

'She was shocked to see him. It's two days running he's come to look at her,' said Sabine. 'I think there's a connection between the two of them.'

'Right. Well, I think I'm going to haul her in,' said Travers.

'I'd rather you didn't,' said Emmett.

'Why?' asked Travers. 'He's dead. What use is she now to you in terms of identifying this man? He's dead. She obviously connected with him. You need to talk to her about that.'

'If it's him,' said Emmett.

'Good ID on him. It'll be him,' said Travers.

'Can I see the room, please?' asked Emmett.

'You can come with me,' said Travers. She escorted Emmett with Sabine in tow over to a hotel and up to a room with some uniformed police officers around it. The rest of the floor was being cleared.

'I'm locking the whole place off. We need to let forensics over the whole place. We're interviewing those in the other rooms,' said Travers.

They put on some coveralls before the forensic officer would let them into the hotel room where the deceased man was found. Standing in the room, they saw a body on the floor. The neck had clearly been twisted and snapped, for it was sitting at an odd angle. Emmett looked down at the face looking back.

The age was right, certainly. He couldn't see any family resemblance, though. Not that there was always one. That was one thing he'd known from his time. You couldn't always say who was related. Sometimes you can make a good guess, but sometimes they look nothing like each other.

'Bought a few items as well, as you can see.'

Emmett looked around. There were various games, cards, tiny figures bought. And Emmett stared at them.

'Gamer like the rest of you, isn't he?' said Travers.

'No, he's not,' said Emmett. 'This is wrong.'

'What do you mean, "Wrong?"'

'No gamer would buy all of this. Nobody who's into Luminite would seriously turn round and buy something from Pavlodimensions. It's just wrong. They don't work in the same systems. It's not the way you would go about things.'

'So, they bought it for somebody else,' said Travers. She was getting agitated with Emmett, and everyone realised it. Sabine was feeling awkward.

'Look,' said Emmett. 'Even the rest of it, those figures don't match up. That figure there and that figure. You paint with that one. This one here's already painted. Why? You wouldn't buy one painted when you buy the unpainted ones. You don't buy painted ones. And you can't strip that one, anyway. It's got the wrong type of paint on it.'

Emmett kept going until Travers put her hand up. 'Stop. Okay, stop. What do you mean, "not a gamer", then? What's the point of all this?'

'All I'm saying,' said Emmett, 'is that this pile of gaming equipment makes no sense. Why is it lying out like this?'

'Often they're very meticulous,' said Sabine. 'Gamers. I know they don't look at this stuff as just stuff. They're meticulous about it. You've painted this, you will hold it, it will be pristine. You will buy it and keep it in its condition. The card games, they put them in little cellophane wrappers to keep them good. You actually buy sleeves for the cards separately,' said Sabine. 'I mean, they don't come with it. You buy them separately. They sit and spend hours putting the cards in. It's something else.'

'What name was the room booked under?' asked Emmett.

'We're just checking that out. I believe it was a Lorraine Harrow.'

'That's odd, isn't it?' said Emmett.

'Using a false name. Turned up as a woman. Clearly didn't want to know somebody was here. It fits the motive of your guy. If he's here to try to see—'

'No, no, no,' said Emmett. 'No, it doesn't. It really doesn't. Our guy has been a drug addict. He has been on the drink. Our guy lives off the streets. Our guy visits a down-on-her-luck woman. That's who his girlfriend was. She was in the rough end of town.

'This guy doesn't come and book a hotel room here. This place would have cost a small fortune, especially with this Expo on. I'm not sure he's got that sort of money. And if he had, he wouldn't be spending it on this. He wouldn't be spending it on games like that. He was a substance misuser. Drug addicts would want drugs. He couldn't afford to do this. This is wrong.'

'Let's have a word with reception then,' said Travers. She tore out of the room as if she expected to be followed and Emmett joined her. Having removed their coverall outfits, they went to the reception and were taken through to the manager.

'A Lorraine Harrow. It was a woman, the staff said.'

'What did she look like?' asked Travers.

'It was Amy who spoke to her. I'll get Amy in.'

A young girl, maybe nineteen, came into the room, dressed in the hotel uniform. She looked nervous, but the manager smiled at her. 'Just tell the police officers what you know.'

'That's right, Amy,' said DCI Travers. 'Just tell me what you know. It's not a problem, but tell me as much as you can, and as accurately as you can. If you're not sure, say you're not sure. Tell me if it's a guess. Tell me if it's what you think, but you're not convinced. Just let me know how it is.'

'Well, she was a tall woman. I think she was maybe five feet ten. Her hair was hard to tell because she had a broad hat on, really large rim to it, and she had sunglasses. She had a scarf too. I don't even know what colour her hair was,' said Amy. 'She checked in with cards and stuff, wrote the address, and that was it.'

'Do you have CCTV?' asked Travers.

'We do,' said the manager.

'Can you take me to it?'

'Can I go and have a look? If that's all right,' Sabine said to Travers.

'Just a moment.' She dialled a number. 'Lonnie,' Travers said, 'I want you to accompany . . .' She stared at Sabine for a moment.

'Detective Sergeant Ferguson.'

'Detective Sergeant Ferguson from Scotland. She's going to look at CCTV. Look at it with her, please, Lonnie.'

'Sabine will give you what you need. It's not a problem,' said Emmett.

'Look,' said Travers, 'it's not that I don't trust you, but you're coming at this from a different place. This is a murder inquiry to me now.'

'Well, I'm running my own murder inquiry.'

'You're running a cold case. This is live, and I may need to act quickly.'

'Of course,' said Emmett. 'It's your investigation. I'm here to give you all the assistance you need.'

Sabine disappeared from the room while Emmett and DCI Travers spoke to the manager. Then Travers spoke to her sergeant who traced the credit card used by Lorraine Harrow. It was based in Switzerland, as was her account, and getting information about it was difficult. Lorraine Harrow had entered the country recently.

By the time Emmett had got round to seeing Sabine again, she had been through most of the day's CCTV, albeit quickly.

'What have you found out, Lonnie?' asked Travers, but Lonnie turned to Sabine. Lonnie was a mid-twenties young man with blond hair who stood nearly six feet tall, and Sabine had found him easy to work with. Now he was letting Sabine speak.

'Well,' said Sabine, 'Lorraine Harrow comes in. You can't see anything of her face from the CCTV . She keeps it away from all the cameras. As she goes through the hotel, the CCTV never picks up her face. The hat is always in the way. She goes into that room. Well, she goes up to the floor, but there's no CCTV on the actual room. Then, she's not seen again. She doesn't leave.'

'She doesn't leave? What does she do? Climb out the window?' asked Travers.

'She either leaves with someone else, or she's found a way out past the CCTV. They didn't set up the CCTV for this to be an impregnable fortress. There'll be a way to get past it without being seen. There'll be other exits.'

'What about our dead body? Does he arrive at some point?'

'I've seen only one thing. There's a glimpse of a grey hood at one of the rear entrances. It's very, very subtle. It's like somebody walking past, trying not to be on the camera. If it were a pair of people,' said Sabine, 'the person in the grey hoodie would be on the outside, somebody else on the inside. The person on the inside doesn't get seen. You get half a head's worth of the grey hood as it goes past. If they hadn't stopped briefly, I wouldn't have noticed it at all.'

'What time's that at?' asked Travers.

'Yesterday, late afternoon after our chase, after we tried to find him. We were still at the expo, looking around.'

'So, you're thinking somebody was brought here?' asked Travers.

'Can I suggest something?' said Emmett. 'When we find out

the identity of the victim, don't release it.'

'What?' said Travers.

'Don't release it.'

'It'd be Alex Baird. You said this was the guy at the NEC. Somebody obviously found him. Somebody obviously isn't happy. I need to interview Orla Jones. I need to talk to her. She's involved in this. Somebody has taken this guy out. She had a shocked expression at seeing him, and someone else had been there and taken him out. A professional, by the look of it. That'll be Alex Baird up there. Somebody's now killed him for a reason.'

'Don't release it when you find out,' said Emmett. 'I'm going to talk to my boss. I need to update him on what's happening. If you need me, I've got my phone.' Emmett turned and walked away, leaving Travers a little bemused. She turned to Sabine.

'Is he always like this? I mean, what on earth's he on?'

'Emmett's a little different,' said Sabine. 'But Emmett's clever. He won't tell you all that's going on in there. But he usually knows what he's on about. Don't release the name. And be careful when you talk to Orla. Don't mention us. Don't mention the other investigations. Play it straight, please.'

'I'll ask what questions I need to sort this out,' said Travers. 'That's my job. I have to sort my case out first.'

'I appreciate that,' said Sabine. 'But please, walk carefully. She doesn't know about us yet. Emmett was dead keen to make sure she didn't. For as long as possible. He's got a reason for that. Trust him on it.'

From the look that DCI Travers gave her, Sabine wasn't sure she'd convinced her.

Chapter 14

We need to identify that man in there,' said Sabine. 'It's key. At the moment, you're saying that's not Alex, but we don't know that. Why don't we just take a photo up to the family? See Gary or Lisa.'

'Because his appearance could have changed,' said Emmett. 'Lisa and Gary haven't seen him for a good while. Who knows what he looked like? The person who knew him best would be Precious. We should go to Precious Hammer. Take a photo of him.'

'Okay. Let's do that then. I take it Travers doesn't want to talk to her.'

'As far as Travers is concerned, she's not linked to him. She wasn't here. So, by the time Travers gets around to talking to her, it could be a couple of days. We'll be doing Travers a favour,' said Emmett.

'Well, let's go then.'

The pair left their hotel and drove to the unit where Precious was being housed. On arrival, she gave a broad smile to Emmett, but he found it difficult to smile back. Taken into her room, they sat down opposite Precious and warned her.

'Going to show you a photograph. It's of a deceased man,'

said Emmett. 'I want to know if you recognise him.'

'Me? Why me? Who is it?'

'We don't know,' said Emmett. 'That's why we're asking. It's not a gory photograph, but seeing a dead person in a photograph is often disturbing. You may need to brace yourself.'

Precious nodded and looked anxious as Emmett took a photograph out of an envelope and placed it in front of her.

'Who's that? I don't know him. I know nothing about him,' said Precious.

'Are you sure?' asked Sabine. 'You've never seen that man.'

'No. That's not Alex. Alex doesn't look like that.'

'Good,' said Emmett. 'I'm glad of that. Sorry to have shown you that.' Stepping outside the room, Sabine looked at Emmett.

'She really didn't know him, didn't she?'

'No' said Emmett. 'That's not him in the hotel.'

'So what? What happened? Why is that man dead, then?'

'I don't know, but it looks like Alex has got away, however he's done it. If he was there looking at Orla, which is what we believe, it looks like he's escaped.'

'But then, who was tailing him, and why? Clearly, somebody wanted to kill him.'

'Well, the other way to read it,' said Emmett, 'is that this would be a totally unrelated murder, and just happened to coincide with us running around looking for people in grey hoodies.'

'Well, I'm not buying that,' said Sabine. She thought for a moment. 'Why don't I get the CCTV from the expo? Get Precious to review it. See if we get a likeness of Alex.'

'That's good,' said Emmett. 'Yes. There's a lot of footage, though.'

'Well, if we think of beforehand, we were scanning, we were all there, and we couldn't find him while he had a hood on. This man who's died is dressed in a hoodie. Could Alex have swapped with him?'

'In which case,' said Emmett, 'he might actually walk around in plain sight. Would have a chance. In fact, would look less conspicuous trying to leave if he didn't have a hoodie on.

'You do that. You look at that CCTV and get it down to Precious,' said Emmett. 'I'm going to pass on the good news to Travers.'

'Don't say it with a smug attitude,' said Sabine.

'What do you mean?'

'You called Macleod out before in cases. You stood toe to toe with him. He wasn't happy, but you were right. We're off-patch here. Travers owes us nothing. Macleod brought you in. You're Macleod's worker. He raised you up when other people wouldn't. That's why he took that from you. Be careful how you talk to her.'

'But she's wrong on this,' said Emmett.

'The rank she's got, the last thing you need to do is go in and tell it to her face in front of everybody. She was pretty determined that was Alex Baird. You're about to say it wasn't. Just take it easy.'

Emmett left in a bit of confusion. He understood people, the way they worked, on many occasions. But when you're in the police force, you were there to detect. You were there to work out what truly had happened. And then arrest or otherwise on that basis.

Therefore, any good detective would want to know the truth, would want to know what had happened. Because if you knew what happened, you could arrest the right people. Now

115

where that information came from would be irrelevant. After all, Emmett saw they were all part of one big team. He had difficulty with people who didn't fall into those lines.

He found Clarissa difficult, but she was there to get to the bottom of it. And for all her stroppiness and for all that she shouted and got on, if you came through with the right answer, if you came through with what had actually happened, she reacted to it and followed it. She was fantastic at swallowing her pride to get the right person, although she more or less shrugged it off, saying that it wasn't actually her being wrong. But whatever, she always made it through.

Macleod backed down when he was wrong and followed you through, backed you up. Travers didn't seem to like Emmett from the start. Maybe it was because Emmett was a gamer. Maybe she'd heard stuff about him. For Emmett knew that in his past, people had found him awkward or just didn't like the way he was. Emmett didn't know why. He didn't bother other people. He just got annoyed with them.

The investigation was still being run at the NEC, and a couple of hotel rooms had been taken over by DCI Travers while they were working on the scene. Emmett flashed his warrant card and got up towards the main room, asking where DCI Travers would be. She was currently with several colleagues going through the case. Emmett knocked on the room door before gaining admittance.

'I'm kind of busy, Inspector,' said the DCI. 'Just running through with the team here.'

'I've got some information that's important,' said Emmett.

'Right,' said Travers. 'If you wait a moment, I'll speak to you just after I finish the brief.'

'You'll need to hear this. It may change what you do.'

He saw Travers look at the other people around her before looking back. 'Well, spit it out then,' she said. Travers was sitting in a trench coat and yet was in a hotel room. Emmett thought it was quite warm. He was standing in his jacket and gaming t-shirt and looked quite diminutive compared to her. She had thick hair despite her years, and whether its flow was natural or the action of some hairdresser, she looked quite formidable.

'I went to see Precious Hammer today.'

'And this is?'

'The woman we told you about, the one who was released from incarceration, that Alex Baird used to go with, his girlfriend.'

'Why?'

'I thought she would know what he looked like. So, I took her a photograph of the deceased man in there.'

'And what?' said Travers.

'It's not Alex. She said it was not Alex.'

'Well, if it's not Baird, who is it?' said Travers suddenly. 'And why are you talking to her? She could be—'

'Well, she couldn't be a suspect,' said Emmett. 'She's not here. She wasn't about the place. She's stuck in a unit. Recovering.'

'She could be important to the case. I'm trying to follow the case through here at the moment. You can't freelance on me.'

'It wasn't freelancing. I'm running a case as well.'

Travers sat back, fuming but thinking. 'Right, then,' she said. 'That changes things. Lonnie?'

'Yes,' said the tall man in the room.

'We need to think about how this person got here, who they are. Let's get some options going about what happened to Alex Baird, if he was even here.'

'I did manage to speak to Orla Jones,' said Travers. 'She told me the man in the hoodie actually had a knife inside his jacket. That's why she looked shocked.'

'What about the first day? How did she explain that one?' asked Emmett.

'Said it was the same man, but he had no knife that day. He was just staring at her in a funny way.'

'So when you showed her the photo of the dead man?—I take it you did that.'

'Of course we did,' said Travers. 'She was relieved. She said she'd felt uncomfortable. But seeing him dead now meant that she was clear he couldn't come after her. Which is pretty reasonable, if you feel threatened like that. Saw someone with a knife. I'm not convinced that your Alex Baird was actually here. It could have been a robbery gone wrong or some sort of action against Orla Jones. Intimidation. We might have to investigate that further. That may be an Alex Baird, who was with this man. Maybe Alex Baird has killed this man. Or maybe it's just two people who blew a robbery or something. Too early to tell.'

'When she was showing the photograph, was there any emotion?' asked Emmett. 'Was there anything on her face to suggest that she knew that person? That she was reacting to their death? That . . .'

'No,' said Travers. 'By the way, when you go to talk to someone, if you don't mind telling me, I may have liked to have been—'

'You should be aware then,' said Emmett, 'that Sabine is currently taking CCTV down to Precious, getting her to look through it to see if we can find if Alex Baird was there.'

'And you're intending to do that how?'

'Precious will identify him. That was the whole point. In case he took off,' said Emmett. 'I'll let you know how that goes.'

'You make sure you do that,' said Travers.

Emmett left a quiet room, feeling awkward. It hadn't gone that well. Did she have a point that he should have spoken to her? Well, he was running a case of his own. They just happened to be overlapping. She hadn't exactly jumped in to help him.

Emmett returned to the unit where Precious was staying and pulled Sabine from the room where she was showing Precious different images.

'How's it going?'

'A lot of footage to see, a lot of things to go through. It's going to take time,' said Sabine. 'She's willing, though. Seems to do a proper job of it. How did it go with Travers?'

Emmett relayed his meeting with Travers, including his doubts that she'd taken it well.

'Is there something in what she's saying, though, about this being something else? About this possibly not being lined up with our case. Or maybe Alex is coming at this from a completely opposite angle.'

'I read this totally differently,' said Emmett. 'I think he was there, and I think he went to Orla for good reasons. She said she saw a knife on the man. No knife was ever found. I think the knife is being brought up by Orla as an excuse for her reaction. I think Alex is about, and I think Orla knows it. All I've got to do is prove it.'

'Well, the only way to prove that Alex is about is to find him. Orla won't tell you if that's the case because clearly there's a reason she doesn't want to meet him. The other thing,' said Sabine, 'is that the man in that room, whoever he is, has been dispatched rather professionally. That's somewhat of a problem because if what you're saying is true, that means somebody has got a hit man or hit woman chasing after Alex. That doesn't bode well.'

'Then we'd better find him quickly,' said Emmett.

Chapter 15

Emmett found a quiet corner of the hotel and placed a call up north to Inverness. As he waited for it to go through, he felt somewhat agitated, and a little nervous. He hadn't, after all, been promoted to DI for that long, and now he was having to work in a world with DCIs with their own problems.

Macleod was easier to work with in some ways. You could challenge him. He didn't take it personally, and he had brought Emmett into the role, so Macleod must have known what Emmett was like. On the other hand, Emmett was having to work with, and he thought possibly having to work around, Travers. He wasn't sure how to do that.

'This is Seoras, Emmett. What do you want? I've got a meeting in about five minutes.'

'I need some advice,' said Emmett.

'You need advice? I don't recall you asking me for advice before.'

'No, but I usually know my mind. I usually know how to get around problems. I'm having a difficult one at the moment.'

'Regarding the case?' asked Macleod.

'Not specifically, but yes. We're having to work with DCI

Travers at the moment because there's been a murder at the hotel near the NEC. Travers has taken on that as her case to investigate. Of course, we're still on the cold case that may be involved in this. But it feels, at times, like it's hard to steer the investigation. She wants to go down one route, and I definitely see other ones.'

'It's two separate investigations, though,' said Macleod. 'Why not just run them like that?'

'We're having to use her people for a lot of what we're doing. It also needs a lot of cross-collaboration, because if the two murders are connected, which I think they may be, we need to treat them like that. We need to look at it from an overall perspective, not just what happened here recently.'

'And have you sat down and talked to Travers about that?'

'I don't think DCI Travers is one of those people.'

'In what way?' asked Macleod.

'I think she has a definite line she wants to go on, and that's where she's going until it proves to be false. She doesn't work openly like me, and I also know that what she's doing isn't right. It's not the right track at the moment. It's—'

'Excuse me,' said Macleod, 'it's not the right track? You definitely know, because if you definitely know, put the evidence in front of her and get her to change track.'

'Well, it's more of a . . . well, it's more than a hunch. I think it's an understanding of the situation. I think it's a . . .'

'Is it something in black and white that will change the opinion of a jury in a court?' asked Macleod.

'No.'

'Well then, you're going to have to work with her. Or around her. Certainly not through her. She holds too high a rank compared to you. But you're not behind the door and calling me out when you think I'm wrong. What's the difference here? She's a DCI as well.'

'You put me in the role I'm in,' said Emmett. 'It's different. I'm giving you what you want, in truth. Giving you that other voice. Giving you that—'

'And you think that just because she didn't put you in place, she will not accept that?'

'I don't think she'll accept it for one minute,' said Emmett.

'Well, if that's the case, you need to take a track that won't collide with Travers, something that won't coincide with what she's investigating. Do it in a way that you're picking up areas she isn't, but don't ram that down her throat. Just see what they bring,' said Macleod. 'Nobody likes a smart cookie after the fact, telling them you should have done what we did.'

'I wouldn't do that,' said Emmett. 'She doesn't understand this gaming community. She doesn't understand—'

'Well, you'll have to enlighten her.'

'The thing is, I want to run a track of hunting down Alex Baird. Now Travers is convinced Alex Baird has just died in that hotel room. I'm convinced he didn't. In fact, we've gone and spoken to Precious, who doesn't recognise the man in there.'

'Have you told her it's not him?'

'I tried to, but now it's a robbery gone wrong. Now it's somebody else. How could the woman tell? I think we can do more with Precious,' said Emmett. 'I think we could get her to look. In fact, I am getting her to look at the CCTV. See if she can recognise Alex out there. But it's going to take time. Sabine's doing that alongside her working the footage over there. I think Sabine connects better with people. She'll also be working with some of DCI Travers's deputies. Keeps me and her apart, out of each other's hair.'

'But if you're going to get a recognised photo or an image, what are you going to do with it?' asked Macleod. 'You know he was an alcoholic or a drug addict. He must have been in recovery groups.'

'Yes, that's true,' said Emmett.

'Well, if he's in groups around Birmingham, do the legwork,' said Macleod. 'Take the image out. See if anybody recognises and knows him. You'll struggle to find him from electoral records or anything like that because he won't be on them. But somebody might recognise him. After all, that's why you went to the expo.'

'On that,' said Emmett, 'Orla Jones said that the man she saw, she didn't recognise, which I don't believe to be true either. Said he had a knife, but no knife was found. It's not making any sense. I'm trying to tell Travers this, but—'

'Don't,' said Macleod. 'If you've got a senior officer going on a different track, you can't just pop in with theories. You've got to come in with concrete evidence that proves they're wrong and then turn around and steer them on the correct track. We're not all as open as I am, not all as ready to take information in.'

Emmett was about to say he didn't do that all the time, but Macleod was coming round to help Emmett, so he thought it better not to say anything.

'So, go out amongst the groups. Do the legwork.'

'I'll need to get some of the uniform sections involved to cover that off. With the number of groups out there, I'm going to need help. I'm going to—'

'No, you're not going to have to go and ask Travers. That's not going to work,' said Macleod. 'She's got a murder case on.

She's going to be pulling everybody she can get. She's going to be searching this, hunting that down. You, however, are going off on a different track. It's not following her track, so she won't give you the people. Therefore, I will.'

'Excuse me?' said Emmett.

'I'll send you the people. I'll send you Perry.'

'Perry? But isn't Perry part of Hope's murder squad? Will Hope be able to cope without him? And I thought Hope was still on maternity anyway.'

'You're actually questioning whether or not I can run the murder squad that I ran for how long before Hope?'

'I'm just saying, you're just throwing people down to me, aren't you?'

'I've got Ross. I've got Susan. If things kick off big time here, I can pull people in. I have got a lot of clout up here. You have got no clout down there. Therefore, I will send the clout from here down to you to be used.'

'Thank you,' said Emmett. 'If he comes into Birmingham NEC, we can pick him up. How long do you think it will take him to get down here?'

'Perry will be there in the morning,' said Macleod. 'But you can start by working out which groups you need to go round. By the sounds of it, Sabine's doing good work, and if she can work well in amongst Travers's lot, keep her there. I was going to suggest Perry, because he'd be good at that too. But, if Sabine's already in and working there, keep her there. Let Perry work with you. He sees things from different angles. He's also very good with people. Going on a hunt for someone, Perry will get you the information. If they're there, I'm sure you'll find them.'

'Okay,' said Emmett. 'I'll work with Perry on that. Hopefully,

Sabine can come up with something as well. Maybe Precious will spot him. Get us a proper photograph.'

'Get the description out anyway,' said Macleod. 'I'm up here if you need me. I'm working especially hard now since I'm a man down. Seems us old people just have to pick up the slack.'

Emmett didn't know if that was a rebuke, and Macleod being Macleod didn't laugh. He hoped it wasn't.

As Emmett closed down the call, he was approached by a uniformed officer advising that DCI Travers wanted to see him. He gave a polite nod, but as soon as the officer's back was turned, he was shaking his head. He didn't need this.

Travers was in the office she'd commandeered in the hotel, and when Emmett went in, she was sitting behind her desk.

'Close the door behind you,' she said.

He did as he was asked. And when he turned back around, Travers was sitting with some photographic images in front of her. They were from CCTV cameras.

'This is from your colleague and my own resourceful underlings,' said Travers. 'They've been going through the expo footage looking for men in hoodies and leather jackets. DS Ferguson's been collating them. But she's telling me that the clarity's not good. Seems there were a number out and about that day. Part of me wonders if that was deliberate. Maybe this was the gang and something went wrong.'

'We got an ID for that dead man yet?' asked Emmett.

'No, we haven't. We're waiting for that. No sign of Lorraine Harrow either.'

'Maybe we should run these past Precious Hammer.'

'Funny,' said Travers. 'DS Ferguson suggested that too. I believe she was taking them there once she'd finished with my lot.'

'Well, that's a line of attack, I guess.'

'Yes. If I could just say something, DI Grump. Obviously, I'm the senior officer here. I've just had a murder in my patch, a very recent murder. We're not chasing down something from family ties from a long time ago. However, I appreciate you have your own case and you think it is linked. I feel that it isn't.

'We haven't got off on the right foot together, though. Therefore, I think we should make a special effort. And that being said, maybe you could inform me more about what you're doing. I wasn't too pleased to hear that the CCTV footage from my investigation is going in front of somebody else on yours. Well, that's fine. I'm happy to share anything. Because if your fanciful idea the cases are connected is right, well then, we'll need to work together, anyway. But maybe more of a heads-up. You might be used to working on your own up there, wherever it is in the wilds of Scotland, but down here, we share information.'

Emmett couldn't help but feel that was actually a rebuke. He felt he was coming in for a ticking off because of what Sabine was doing. It would be hard to tell Sabine off. After all, she was working through CCTV footage and sharing it, and working alongside Travers's people. Sabine was so good at that. She was incredibly easy-going. And although Emmett knew she got on with him, he knew he was awkward at times. Sabine seemed to get on with everyone, even Clarissa. The Northern Irish woman was something else.

'Well, I'll try to keep you up to date with what I'm doing, and if you could do the same for me, I would appreciate that greatly,' said Emmett, through clenched teeth.

'Excellent,' said Travers. With that, she put her head down, looking at paperwork, and Emmett believed he was dismissed. He went off to find Sabine, who was just finishing up for the day. She was heading out to her car so she could go to meet Precious Hammer, with many of the photographs and images she'd had blown up into fixed frames.

'There you are,' she said to Emmett. 'I've been going through CCTV like anything. Got something for Precious to look over. Just on my way there now. You coming?'

'Yes. I also had a word with DCI Travers. Or rather, she pulled me in. She seems to think that we should run almost everything through her. We should be—'

'Just keep her informed. That's all she's looking for. Gets us out of her hair as soon as I inform her what's going on and why it's going on. But then maybe I'm just an underling.'

'In that case, you can drive,' said Emmett.

They headed for the car and, on arrival at the unit where Precious was staying, they were directed up towards her room. She had a smile when she opened the door to see them, but then when they pulled out the brown envelope with lots of photographs in it, she looked less excited.

Sabine sat down with her, passing each image before her. Most of them were from funny angles, clarity often poor, blurriness being a major feature. Precious went through them over and over, giving a few maybes, which were then put aside to be brought out at the end of the run-through. But then, Precious suddenly pointed.

'That one there—that's him. That's Alex.'

Emmett looked at the photograph. It was the back of a man.

'Why do you think it's him?' asked Sabine.

'The stance, the posture, that's him.'

It got no better. Sabine kept going with the photographs.

And in the end, there were a couple of images that were maybes. There was only one definite one. But it was an image that was from behind.

'But she says it's his shape. I mean, that's fair enough. He's dressed the right way; it's his shape,' said Sabine.

'Travers won't buy that as a positive ID. There's no way. It doesn't suit what she wants either. Therefore, she won't follow it. The subconscious will be pulling her away from it. I spoke to Macleod. We need to get real hard evidence in front of her if she's going to change her mind, if we're going to drive her along our track. Besides, I've got a plan. Perry's joining us.'

'Perry?' said Sabine.

'Perry and I are going to chase up all the places that Alex could have gone. We'll take his description and maybe his shape in the photograph here with us. Good old-fashioned legwork, Macleod called it. That's why he's sending Perry. He says, you're to stick close to the investigation here that Travers is running.'

'Cheers. I'm working the hard road and you're already offloading me as a partner.'

'Just make sure we get it done,' said Emmett. Clearly, he wasn't in the mood to be poked.

Chapter 16

'So which train did you say Perry was coming in on?'

'Crewe,' said Sabine. 'Took the overnight sleeper. Got off at Crewe. He'd have been off that about half five this morning. He'll be here any time now.'

Emmett sat on the platform at a small table, having coffee with Sabine. The station at the NEC had rather large platforms, which, at times, seemed ridiculous. But he guessed there must have been some volume of traffic through, especially with the expo.

'So, Macleod said that you and he were to go around the groups in the Birmingham area.'

'That's what he said. Keep me out of Travers' hair.'

'You don't want to be doing this if Perry's down. He's a constable; I'm a sergeant. We can cover that. Besides, I haven't got any more CCTV to go through. I'm kind of done with Travers's lot. We know what we've got from it. Precious has identified him, albeit from his figure, not his face. This is the line of attack.'

'There's another line of attack,' said Emmett.

'What?'

'Well, the hotel. I was thinking if we look at the guest list at the hotel, we maybe should have a look at everybody who's there, where they've come from.'

'Because?'

'Well, the woman with the enormous hat who booked the room that the body was disposed in, how did she get out of that room? Is it a room that she used when, shall we say, anything went wrong? If you arrived as a certain person and checked in and then left as that person, you would remain pretty anonymous. Except you then drop a body in there because you have to go out quickly. If you have two rooms and have two separate people booked in, or at least one person pretending to be two different people, that would allow you to set that room up. Give you a way of presenting it the next day while you had already left. You could check out, be gone before the body's discovered.'

'You think of that on your own?'

'Yes,' said Emmett. 'Why?'

'It's pretty devious. You're talking about someone setting up a contingency.'

'If somebody was after Alex Beard, they could be people with money, such as those who founded the game Majik Falls. In which case they send a professional, somebody who does plan ahead, does keep themselves covered, and knows how to get out quickly. But also, someone who could be on a watchlist for coming into the country. They might not know exactly who they are. And I thought if I talked to Border Control and others, we could see if that digs anything up.'

'Isn't this much more what Travers should be doing?' asked Sabine. 'Or at least you could take it to her and see if she would do it.'

'I need to move quick,' said Emmett. 'She gets bogged down.

131

I don't think she wants to use me as an extra. You, no problem. I'm running the other case. And I think she wants them to be kept separate at the moment. I don't think they are separate. It makes sense for me to do this on my own, and if it gets somewhere, at least we are not behind the drag curve of the killer.'

'I think it'll also cheese off Travers if you do that.'

'Macleod said I needed to give her something concrete to get her to change track. I'm going for something concrete, but this is the only way I know how to do it. So, you two do that spade work. Macleod said Perry was excellent at it. You are too. Good with people. You'll get them talking. I'm not. It's not me. It's not how I work. I'm not—'

'No, you're not,' said Sabine.

'Well, thank you for the vote of confidence,' said Emmett.

'It's just honest,' said Sabine. 'Oh, look, the train's coming.'

The pair stood up and then scanned the platform as the doors of the train opened. At the far end, Sabine saw Perry get out. He almost half-moseyed out with his rucksack carelessly hung around his shoulder. Perry was wearing flannel trousers, a jacket, and a shirt without a tie. He looked his usual unkempt self but he gave a broad smile as he spotted Sabine.

'Hi there,' he said, approaching. He put out his hand to shake Sabine's, but she stepped forward and gave him a hug. 'Good to see you, Perry,' she said. 'You're with me today.'

'I always get to work with a younger woman,' said Perry. 'Must be the figure.'

Emmett reacted for a moment. He always struggled when other people talked about Sabine. But she was smiling.

'Hey, if he wants to call me the younger woman,' she said to Emmett, obviously picking up his distress, 'he can come and work with me any day. It's only Susan who normally gets called the younger woman. At least, the last time I got called it I was working with Clarissa.'

'You and Sabine are going to do some hunting for me. Sabine will bring you up to speed,' said Emmett. 'I've got something else to do.'

'As you wish, boss,' said Perry.

'You don't want a coffee or anything?' said Sabine. 'You've been on the go forever.'

'Let's get going,' said Perry. 'Job to do. If he sent me down, there's a job to do. Let's go do it.'

Emmett watched the two of them disappear and noticed how they talked away the whole time as they climbed up the stairs to leave the platform. Emmett almost felt a little jealous of that. He and Sabine got on well, but Perry just seemed to have ease when he talked to anyone. He could get them talking. Macleod was right. That's the type of guy he was, and yet, he looked like everything a good-looking man wasn't.

Emmett returned to the hotel, taking a room set aside for the police. He sat down at a telephone and called a contact he had at border control. They were able to look at departures from the country for him. Emmett pulled out the guest list he had. There were a few foreign guests, but only a handful of them were women. It was a woman they were looking for. And so, he passed on their details.

'Well,' said the contact, 'most of them have gone back, routine short visits. One I've got here is a Heidi Schmidt, but she's not returned. Do you want me to look more into that?'

'Please,' said Emmett and sat there waiting for the response to come back.

'Okay, Heidi's passport shows that she'd never travelled

133

to the UK before. She's previously been to other countries including African countries, and South American countries.'

'Interesting,' said Emmett.

'Interesting?'

'Why is she travelling there?'

'Some of these countries are on our lists of not quite people to watch, but of questions to be asked. That's how we say "Stop them and talk to them. Find out what's going on." Let's have a look. Yes, they had a brief interview with her but nothing untoward.'

'Can you send me the photograph from the passport?'

'Of course,' said his contact.

Emmett got the photo sent through to his phone and then went off to look at the CCTV footage of the hotel. Travers's people had been through it already, and Emmett had to grab one of the hotel staff to show him how to operate the system. The footage was all about to be sent away, but Emmett hung on to it and began checking through it.

It took the best part of the morning and into the afternoon before he saw Heidi Schmidt at reception. She had her head turned away from the camera. She was checking in after Lorraine Harrow had booked in, which made sense. If you were living a double life, the first one would check in, you'd dress and change into the other outfit, and then you would come in and book again.

What also interested Emmett was that the head was away from the camera. It was definitely her. He began scanning through, and once again, Heidi could be seen several times through the day at the hotel, coming in and leaving again. In each one, she was keeping a distinct look away from the main cameras.

Then Emmett noticed that although she kept avoiding the camera, in one image he could see a couple with a man filming the woman. They looked in their sixties, and he thought they must have been tourists. The man was filming when the woman was talking on camera, and right behind her was Heidi Schmidt. In fact, Schmidt seemed to get annoyed at suddenly realising the camera was on her, but off she went.

The door of the CCTV suite burst open. 'My people have already gone through this. Why on earth are you looking over it again? We're going to tag it all into the investigation. You can have all the footage you want, but what are you looking at?'

'I'm looking at a bit of a hunch.'

'I don't think it was worth—we talked about this. We talked about you coming and telling me what you were doing.'

'I know, but it is a hunch.'

'It's a hunch that's had you in there all day. If it was a hunch, surely it would be something quick.'

'Just an idea I've had about the room where our man was murdered.'

'What about it?'

'Think about it,' said Emmett. 'If you were coming here to kill him, or to kill someone who looked like him—'

'Assassination? You've got assassination on the cards? That's a bit of a jump. Looks more like something gone wrong.'

'I know you're of that opinion,' said Emmett, 'but trust me, go with me on what I'm saying. If it were a potential takedown, you would come here knowing you're doing that job. Nothing to stop you coming in and booking a second room so you can change disguise, stay in it, or you can operate out of it while leaving somebody in the other room. If you've got a body to dispose of, you've got to work out how to do it. Maybe our killer did it by planting all that gaming stuff. This was their way of trying to explain it not as being done by a hitman or woman but done in the course of normal criminal events.'

'It's a heck of a jump,' said Travers, 'but it's your time, so you can look through it, but just tell me next time, okay? I've just been told that we can't shift CCTV footage. We can't take away the systems because DI Grump is the one who wants them. But DI Grump needs to come and see me. This is all about my murder case. I know you've got your own to run, and if any information comes up that's solely about yours, you will have complete jurisdiction over it. You'll decide where it goes. But with this lot, it's mine and I do. You need to talk to me. Anyway—'

She turned on her heel and walked out, leaving Emmett a little discombobulated. She was probably right, though. He looked up on the screen and saw the man and the woman, with Heidi behind her. It was a direct line, wasn't it? Her face was always held away from the camera, but this was a camera she wasn't expecting.

Emmett made his way down to the staff at reception. He'd taken a photograph of the image he'd pulled up on the CCTV screen and asked the staff if they knew who this couple was. There were phone calls sent back to people who were now at home, having worked that day. But after an hour, Emmett had his answer. An American couple. He asked the hotel for details, and they were able to give him the phone number the man had given. He had a home address in America, but Emmett wasn't sure if he'd left and gone back there yet, so he took the mobile number and called it.

'Hello?'

'Oh, good afternoon, sir. I'm here to ask something from you. My name is Detective Inspector Emmett Grump. You were at the NEC and specifically at one of the NEC hotels when we found a dead body in a room.'

'Happened when we were right there.'

'Well, I'm with the British Police, and I'd like to talk to you and your wife, and also maybe pick up some film footage that you took.'

'Film footage? I was taking film of my wife. She likes to talk about the places we are, giving all the history and all the bumph,' he said. 'It's a pain in the arse.'

'That may be, but I need to come and talk to you.'

'That's all right. You can come and deal with an issue for us as well.'

Emmett was shaking his head. The guy didn't get how this worked. Emmett would be asking all the questions. He wasn't there to field any from them. He'd have to work out how to put that politely, but firmly.

'Well, we moved on down the road. We're still in Birmingham.' The man gave the address of a different hotel.

'I'll be over directly,' said Emmett. 'I take it that's where you are at the moment.'

'Yeah, that's where we are. But the wife's in the shower at the moment. So, take your time. You're not getting in the room while she's in there.'

Emmett wondered if the man had trouble with this before. It seemed a strange thing to say.

'No problem, sir. I'm on my way.'

Chapter 17

'How are you still going?' asked Sabine. Perry smiled back at her. The sweat was dripping off him.

'Police work is what we do. Good shoes,' said Perry. 'Always good shoes. It doesn't matter what else. The rest of you can look a mess, but the shoes have to be good because you're on your feet all the time. Learnt that in Glasgow.'

'From Macleod?'

'No,' said Perry. 'No idea what Macleod wears on his feet. Macleod back then wouldn't have bothered answering trivial stuff like that for you. He's a bit more open these days, but he will not talk to you about your shoes or how you look and dress. And saying that, I wouldn't take a fashion tip from him—a man that has only shirts and ties and trousers.'

Sabine looked at Perry and wondered just exactly who he took fashion tips from and whether she could avoid them.

'Doesn't it get you down though?' said Sabine. 'We're walking around all these places and everywhere, you've got recovery groups. You've got Alcoholics Anonymous. Drug rehabilitation. Financial difficulties. How many people are under the cosh? How many people have made a mess of it?'

'Well, that is true,' said Perry. 'I didn't think of it like that. I don't get down. I try to see the people who are there. Get their actual stories. Many people are there for excellent reasons. Not pleasant reasons, but good reasons. And well, you've just got to help them, haven't you? Whereas other people are there because of ignorant fault or deliberate abuse of themselves. What are you going to do? Jump all over them? Whether somebody sorts themselves out is not up to me. I've got a job to do. Get on with it and just try to deal with people as best you can.'

They were currently on the south side of Birmingham and in a rather run-down area.

'Well, that's the next one up there,' said Perry. He looked at the graffiti around the building it was located in. Some of it was rather rude and, frankly, quite unimaginative.

'I used to see graffiti sometimes,' said Perry, 'and I thought, *our kids have got an amazing talent*. But some of these, they've just got no talent. Look at that, I mean, seriously, would you want that?' Perry stopped.

He realised that while it was rude, it certainly wasn't something that Sabine wanted and certainly shouldn't have been about. She gave a laugh.

'It's okay,' she said. 'I know what you're saying. No, but I guess it's hard to pick people up. The system's struggling too. When you're young, there's help for you. When you're old, there's no help. That's why you get all these volunteer groups, charities, everything. We've got to look after our own, Perry. Do it better.'

'We're getting into some sort of political debate here.'

'Can't help it,' said Sabine. 'Come on. We'll do this one, and then we're going to get something to eat.'

'There's been nothing so far. I thought for a guy who was an

139

addict, he'd have cruised round all of these groups, especially if Precious said he was getting help.'

'Well, what he told Precious and what actually happened could be two different things. I mean, at the end of the day, he was trying to impress her. Trying to win her over.'

'Well, that's an inauspicious start if he's lying to her. There's no point. No point in all that nonsense. They find out in the end, don't they?'

'I'm not actually one of your male colleagues,' said Sabine. 'I'm not sure you're meant to offer that statement at me.'

Perry looked somewhat sheepish. 'Susan doesn't mind these things.'

'Anyway,' said Sabine, 'I heard you had some woman issues in the past.'

Perry smiled. 'Things are better,' he said. 'I took Tanya out the other night, properly. Like on a date. Susan's, well, we're colleagues. We're working away together. That's it. I don't know. Everything got a bit nuts there with that last job we were all involved in. When they tried to kill Tanya, and I had to save her, I think maybe brought her closer to me, something I didn't realise. I think Tanya's been the one all along.'

'Well, I guess you're closer in age.'

'That never bothered me. I mean, not unless it looked really dodgy, but it didn't, you know. Susan's a grown woman—I'm a man. There's not that many years between us—ten, fifteen, something like that. Tanya's . . . well . . . .Tanya's more me.'

'I'll wish you the best of luck with that,' said Sabine.

'What about you?' said Perry.

'What about me?'

'Well, you know, got anyone in your life?'

'And why would I tell you?' asked Sabine.

'Well, you just chimed in about mine. The least you can do is return the favour,' smiled Perry.

'No, there's no one,' said Sabine.

Perry stopped and stared at her.

'What?' I said. "There's no one."'

'Do I have to call you a liar?' asked Perry.

For a moment, Sabine folded and then she spat back with, 'You will, yes.'

'Liar,' said Perry.

'Why'd you say that?'

'Do you know if he's interested?' said Perry suddenly.

'Who?'

'This person in your life.'

'It's hard to tell,' said Sabine. 'I think so, but I don't know. It's hard to tell.'

'Swapping around your positions must have made it awkward. I mean, under Clarissa, you'd have been the expert. Now, he's the boss. Working together on a team, it's not simple. You're wondering whether the affection's coming from that. The closeness of how you're working, or whether it's actually genuine. I feel for you,' said Perry.

Sabine stopped. She looked at him. 'Is it that obvious?'

'That's a redundant question to me. I find a lot of things obvious that other people don't. Anyway, like you said to me, all the best for that.'

Perry turned almost with a smug look on his face, knowing he'd found out the truth as ever. Sabine was blushing red, but she followed him and entered a large building that had a drug recovery group advertised outside. As they walked in, they were approached by a caretaker who pointed them down the hall to where there were a couple of small offices.

'Are you looking for someone?' said a voice from down the corridor.

'We're looking for the person who runs the drug recovery group.'

'That'll be me. I'm Eamon. Is there something I can do to help you?'

'DS Ferguson,' said Sabine, pulling out her warrant card. 'This is DC Perry. We're wondering if you've ever seen this person here.' Sabine took out an artist's impression of the description that Precious had given the team of Alex. She saw the man step back suddenly.

'Wow,' he said. 'I recognise that face alright. It's Alex.'

'Alex who?' asked Perry.

'He didn't give me a second name. Just called Alex.'

'And how long has he been coming here?'

'Three months or around that. At least. He's not on the books with me as a client, so to speak. He just comes to the drop-in. But I've got talking to him. Guy with a real chip on his shoulder. Quite angry.'

'Is he definitely on drugs?' asked Perry.

'Oh yes. He's come in here sometimes high as a kite. But also, when he talks about other things, he can't get his act together at all. Curls up into a wee ball sometimes when his fears strike. Other times he's here looking pretty normal.'

'Did he mention someone called Precious?'

'A woman? Not by the name Precious. No, he mentioned a woman. She was a black woman, though. I know he said that. He said he wasn't sure how family would take to that.'

'Did he ever talk about his family?' asked Sabine.

'Never said where he came from. Never said why he was in the situation he was in. We're very cautious. Very careful about how we do this. Take time with people. Sometimes they need a bit of space before they open up. But three months is a lot of space.'

'So when you say he's come here for three months, what day of the week is that? Or days?'

'I've got a drop-in open all week, and it can vary when he comes in. But can I know why you are asking me this? The other officer asked me all about it already.'

'The other officer. What officer?' asked Perry.

'We had a detective constable come in here.'

'Did they have a warrant card?'

'A warrant card?' said the man.

'Yes, the card I showed you,' said Sabine. And Perry pulled his out to remind the man.

'Eh, I don't think I looked for it. I don't know whether or not she had one. Just wondered why you guys weren't talking to each other.'

'Well, do you know her name?' asked Perry.

'Began with an L. No, no. Hang on. I just need to check my office. I took her name down.' He disappeared into his office and then came back. 'Lauren Shea. Do you know her?'

Perry looked at Sabine and shook his head. Sabine shook back.

'Tell you what,' said Perry. 'I'm just going to disappear from the conversation for a moment. I need to check up on something.' As he walked past Sabine, he whispered in her ear. 'I'll phone Tanya. I want to see if there's a Lauren Shea on the force or not.'

'Good idea. I'll keep going with him.' Perry disappeared out of the room, picked up his phone and called Tanya.

'Well, it went so well the other night,' she said, that you just disappear off, run south of the border. Somebody told me you were off working with that younger woman.' Perry had barely said hello and Tanya was all over him. He liked it.

'I'm working with Emmett and Sabine. And while Sabine is a younger woman, she's not that much younger. Though she does like me to call her a younger woman,' said Perry.

'Perry, you call her what?'

'Don't panic,' he said. 'It's just a joke she was having. Anyway, I'm calling because I need something from you.'

'I thought you were calling to tell me you miss me,' said Tanya.

'If I need to call you to tell you that, you're not picking up the signal,' said Perry. 'I need to know if there is a DC Lauren Shea on the force. Anywhere in the UK.'

He heard a grunt on the phone. Tanya disappeared off the phone for a few minutes, but then came back to say, 'No, no DC Lauren Shea on the force. Scotland or England or Wales, not even Northern Ireland.'

'They've been going around investigating down here, flashing cards. That's not good.'

'So where are you taking me when you come back?' asked Tanya.

'Sorry,' said Perry, 'I'm not with it. I need to think about this one. I'll try to call you tonight.'

'Okay, got what you wanted, off you go.'

It wasn't like that. Perry just needed to run down a thought when it came to him. He hoped Tanya would understand. Perry closed the call, then found Sabine still talking to the group leader. When she'd finished, they stepped outside of the building.

'Did he say anything else?'

'Said the guy was quirky. T-shirts with films and other things, that's all. What about you? How did you get on?'

'There is no DC Lauren Shea, not on the force. So, what do we do then?' asked Perry.

'Well, one thing we can do is hunt down the CCTV cameras around here, see if we can find our man on the move. Possibly also be looking for some CCTV cameras further out in the streets. But if he's coming here, and he's been coming here for three months, there's a good bet we might see him.'

'He's also been here recently,' said Perry. 'Maybe that's why we couldn't find him the other day, but he is definitely active at the moment.'

Sabine looked around trying to pick out where there would be CCTV to capture Alex entering the building. Meanwhile, Perry called Emmett with the good news, and Emmett congratulated them on an excellent piece of work. Sabine walked up and down, noting the cameras, prepping herself for asking to get some images.

'You didn't tell me something about the other night,' said Sabine, suddenly.

'What?' asked Perry.

'You didn't tell me whether she enjoyed it. I mean, where did you take her?'

'Well, she said she wanted something simple. So I did. We got takeaway.'

'Takeaway? You're going out on a date, and you got a takeaway?'

'We don't do big-style stuff, you know. I mean, we're past that. Well down the line. I just want to see if we get along with each other. There's no point in being somebody different. She actually likes my style. It's not like I need to change it for her.

'That's a lot. It's an awful lot in life. If you can be yourself and that one you like, that partner likes you for being it. If you can like them for being that way too, that's nearly a match made in heaven,' laughed Perry. Sabine stopped, and Perry noticed.

'Problem?' he said. 'That other person does not quite fit that bill? Something wrong with him? You tried to change them?'

'No,' said Sabine. 'I was going along thinking, *it's a marvellous idea and it can't work*. The problem with you, Perry, is every time I talk to you, you seem to convince me it can.'

'Best I shut up then,' said Perry and laughed.

Chapter 18

'Not at the moment, son, we're waiting for a police officer. Whatever it is you've got for us, it can wait until another time.'

The man had broad shoulders, was fairly tubby and was losing his hair on top. *You have glasses that are big enough to cover ten eyes and a rather flashy wristwatch,* Emmett thought. He'd come looking for the couple who had filmed the mysterious woman, Heidi Schmidt. They were in a different hotel now, but not that far away, and Emmett was meeting them for the first time.

'I think you misunderstand, sir,' said Emmett, and reached inside his jacket, taking out his warrant card. 'I'm DI Emmett Grump. The police officer?'

'You don't look like a police officer.'

'No, I'm a detective. We don't dress in the uniform. Not usually when we're working.'

'Oh, you're like our detectives, but most of them go like shirt and tie or something. Gotta look smart.'

Emmett put the warrant card away without bothering to reply to that.

'Is your wife about?' he asked.

'She is indeed. It's Amy Lou,' he said, pointing over to a woman who looked like she was in her sixties, but with long, blonde, immaculate hair and a bright disposition. 'And I'm Douglas Johns III.'

'What is it exactly you want from us?' Amy Lou had arrived now, and Emmett put out his hand to shake hers.

'Thank you for speaking to me, ma'am,' said Emmett. 'To answer your question, what we need to do is get the footage from the camera that you've been filming with, specifically from a time when you were staying near the NEC. In that hotel? You were in the lobby filming. I need to see that footage.'

'Why? What have we done?' asked Douglas Johns.

'You have done nothing, sir. It's what's going on in the footage's background. You may have inadvertently captured an image of someone we need to talk to. So, I need your footage.'

'So, it's not us at all?'

'No, sir. I don't think you've done anything wrong.'

'No, we have done nothing wrong,' laughed Amy Lou. 'But it's a good job you came because we've been wronged.'

'In what way?' asked Emmett.

'Some bastard took my camera,' said Douglas. 'Standing there, filming Amy Lou with it. Next thing, put it down, and it was gone.'

'You've lost the camera,' said Emmett.

'I didn't say lost. I said it was stolen.'

'Have you reported this to our police already?'

'Going down to do that today. It only happened this morning.'

'Did you get a look at whoever took it?' asked Emmett.

'No, I told you. I just put it down, turned around, and then it was gone.'

'And gone from where?'

'We were outside,' said Amy Lou. 'Out in town, close to here. In fact, it's just around the corner.'

'Can you show me?' asked Emmett.

'Why?' asked Douglas. 'There's nothing in particular. It's . . .'

'Can you just show me, please?' asked Emmett.

The man nodded, and the three of them made their way out onto the Birmingham streets. It was a rather dull day, but the walk was short. There was a small, almost oasis-like patch of green grass with some benches around it, stuck away in the middle of the cityscape.

Douglas walked over to the middle of it, and pointed to one of the benches. There was another man sitting there at that moment. He edged across gently as Douglas pointed at him.

'That's where it was, right there where that fella's sitting.'

'There's no need for alarm, sir,' said Emmett to the man. 'The gentleman's just showing me where he had something stolen from him. We're not looking in your direction at all. Sorry to bother you.'

The man gave a bit of a nod but then seemed more appeased when Emmett produced his warrant card.

'So just tell me exactly what you were doing,' said Emmett.

'We were here,' said Douglas. 'Amy Lou was there. I was filming because we got that lovely background there. I put the camera down and then I went to get something out of my pocket. Turned back for the camera, and it was gone.'

'And did you see anyone?'

'We saw lots of people,' said Amy Lou. 'I wasn't looking at the time. I was looking over there. But I turned around and there's lots and lots of people.'

'Did you shout at all? Did you?'

'No. At first, I thought I'd just dropped it under the bench or something,' said Douglas. 'I went down, had a look around. And then, well . . .'

'Did you stop anyone? Ask anyone?'

'We stopped a few people. They said to tell the police. Just to report it.'

'You should have worn the hand strap like I told you,' said Amy Lou. 'You should have worn that one.'

'Oh, give it a rest, woman. Oh, she's been at me ever since I lost that camera. You should have worn this. You should have worn that.'

'Well, I was right, wasn't I?' said Amy Lou.

'Can we just calm down a minute?' said Emmett, a little taken aback by the fervour of the couple towards each other. 'The people that were here, anybody stand out? Did you think anybody was close by you at any time today?'

'No, if I had thought that, I would have told you. I would have said to you, there's this person or whatever, but no. No idea. We weren't that long out of the hotel when we came round here. We'd only gone for a short walk.'

Emmett looked around him. There was no CCTV looking down on this part of the city. CCTV everywhere, but not here. *This is deliberate*, he thought. *This wasn't somebody just randomly grabbing a camera. This was someone who probably waited. Did she know? Did Heidi Schmidt know she was in the background? But she had to wait for her moment, had to follow them.*

'Where have you been in the last few days?' asked Emmett.

'We haven't been anywhere. Douglas has been ill. We were at that hotel back at the NEC. We left that. Douglas wasn't feeling well, but we got to the new one here. He's been up in his room. I have been out.'

'Did you take the camera with you at all?' asked Emmett.

'No. I don't know how to operate that darn thing.'

'She doesn't. She's clueless about it,' said Douglas.

'Well, thanks for that,' said Amy Lou. 'You don't have to tell everyone.'

'You just told them, woman.'

'Again, can we calm down?' said Emmett. 'So that camera hasn't been out of your sight since the hotel at the NEC?'

'It was in my bag when I travelled here. We got a taxi; we went straight here,' said Douglas.

So, this has been the first chance, thought Emmett. *The first chance for the camera to be grabbed. She's been following them. She's worried, but the camera's gone.* Emmett wanted to punch something. Anything.

'Looks like you can't help me then,' said Emmett.

'Why's that?' said Douglas.

'Your camera—it's gone. I take it you were putting the film onto a card or whatever in the back of the camera? Were you using the same one?'

'Yeah, there's one in the back of the camera,' said Douglas. 'But I don't trust them things. Mine uploads. It uploads straightaway. Doing it all the time. Anything new that comes in, it just starts feeding it up to the cloud.'

Emmett felt buoyed suddenly. 'What? Up to the cloud,' he said. 'You mean . . .'

'Yeah. We got all our stuff. It's the camera that's a pain in the ass. It's gone. Bloody gone now, isn't it?'

'Are you insured?' asked Emmett.

'Yeah, of course.'

'Well, you have lost little then,' he said. 'I'm sorry they took it from you, but at the end of the day, you'll get your camera back on the insurance.'

'You saying you won't be able to find it?'

'If the person I think has taken it, that camera will be destroyed and everything inside it.'

'Well, that's a shame, but I guess it's to be expected.'

'What I need to do is talk to you about your account and where those images are. We need to secure them straightaway.'

'Well, how are you going to do that?'

'Back to the hotel,' said Emmett.

He arrived back at the hotel with Douglas and Amy Lou and at first thought he would sit them down in the lobby. Then he thought about going to their room. Most of what was there—anything he was uploading or working on—wouldn't be seen by anyone else. But it was a bit much to invade their room.

Emmett went over to reception, explained a little of the situation and asked if he could borrow one of their conference rooms. He was shown to a room with an internet connection and then brought Douglas and Amy Lou inside. He arranged for coffee and food for them and then sat beside them.

'It's up in this cloud account here,' said Douglas. The man had a laptop with him, opened it up and logged in. Once he'd done so, he went through, pointing out the different footage. Emmett worked out the time and the date of the footage he needed and then allowed Douglas to find those particular images. When he'd done so, Emmett sat and watched the recording play with Douglas.

'That's Amy Lou in the background. I'm just filming her there. She comes across. We liked it because we think there's a bit of history in that hotel.'

Emmett inside was shaking his head. *There's no history at that hotel. There's nothing*, he thought. *Why on earth?* But then he focused back on what he was looking at. There was a woman in the background, drifting this way and that. But then he saw her, looking over the shoulder of Amy Lou. It was only a few seconds. It was brief, but it was a clear facial image.

'That one,' said Emmett. 'I need that one, Douglas. Let's download that.'

Emmett had it sent to his phone from Douglas, and he then uploaded it to his own cloud where the team could access it. He thanked the couple, took their details in case he needed to contact them again, and then sent the image to his border force contact. He sat having a coffee, waiting for them to get back to him. An hour later, they came back with bad news. They didn't know the woman. No details on her at all.

Emmett was frustrated. He decided he would go back to his own hotel, wait to see what the other two were doing. It was only an hour later when Sabine got back, along with Perry.

Sabine had collected CCTV footage from a street near the drug recovery group. She relayed to Emmett how a DC Lauren Shea had been ahead of them and asked to watch some images on her laptop. She played for him footage that she'd found of Lauren Shea. Looking at it, Emmett compared the image he had and ran his video longer, trying to get an idea of the height of the woman. The woman in his footage had the right shape to be the same person as in Sabine's footage. She had the right height from what he could judge.

The person who took the camera may have been Lauren Shea as well. He knew the person who'd taken the camera was there that morning in Birmingham. Apparently, she'd visited the drug recovery group, but not that day, but on previous days. Emmett sat pondering what it all meant.

Perry was sitting beyond Sabine and Emmett, who had plonked themselves together on chairs looking at the laptop. They were in Emmett's room, so Perry was standing over by the window, not wanting to sit on anything.

'Just a thought,' said Perry.

'A thought,' said Emmett. 'That sounds ominous.'

'You said that this woman, she turns away, doesn't put her face towards anything. We've said that she's gone looking for Alex. She also doesn't come up on any of Border Force's checks. How has she got into the country then? If she's meant to have shown passports, does she disguise herself? Does she move around without people knowing? And she's hunting Alex,' Perry reiterated. 'That says to me we may have a hitwoman on our hands.'

Emmett looked at Sabine, and she gave a nod. 'You could be right. It's where you were going anyway, wasn't it? It's what you thought all along.'

'I thought they'd sent someone,' said Emmett. 'But a hit woman. I mean, someone to actually take him out, not just scare him off, not just threaten him, not just—'

'Why would you threaten him if he knows so much about the death of his father? I mean, that's what it's got to be about, isn't it? What else has he got? What else has he got that people need to get worried about?' said Perry.

'I think we need to make a call and talk to the big boss,' said Emmett. 'Macleod, he's got a lot more experience of this sort of thing. I may need a lot more clout if this is what's happening.'

'Well, it's never a poor decision to bring him in,' said Perry.

Chapter 19

Susan Cunningham was sitting in front of Macleod, and he thought she looked rather glum. He was a floor down from his own in Hope's office, covering for her while she was on maternity leave, but thankfully the murder squad were quiet at this time. He was running over some of the old cases, tying things up, preparing statements that needed to be made. All the extra work that goes into the prosecution of criminals, which comes after the work of catching them in the first place, has been done.

'You missing Perry or something?' said Macleod suddenly. 'You look so morbid. It's not like you. The first time I saw you, I thought, she's got a magnificent smile,' said Macleod. He saw Susan look up almost in shock.

'You don't normally say things like that,' she said. 'How bad am I?'

'It's the sort of thing Hope might say,' said Macleod. 'I'm covering for her, so I've got to pick the team up the way she would.'

Susan stared at him, then realised he was cracking a joke. She gave a small chuckle before resuming her gloomy posture.

'What's up then? You're clearly out of sorts.'

'It's nothing, nothing I need to get into,' she said.

'It is something you need to get into. It'd be easier with Hope, wouldn't it?'

'Frankly, yes.'

'What's wrong? Is it anything to do with the job?' asked Macleod.

'Well, not really, no.'

'So it's someone in the job. It must be—ah!' said Macleod. He thought about Tanya upstairs. Tanya seemed on cloud nine at the moment. Susan was looking down. Perry had seemed less indecisive lately. Not that Macleod had asked him about his current relationships. Macleod didn't want to go there. But at the moment, Susan clearly could use a friend.

'You want to talk about it?' he said.

'What's there to talk about? She's got him, and I'm left. Well, I blew it, didn't I? He was all over me. He wanted to be with me. Then he goes down to Glasgow, finds her, brings her back up because they used to have something, and now he's had to decide.'

'Yes,' said Macleod, 'and he's made it.'

'That's it. That's your comforting arm, is it?' said Susan.

'Frankly,' said Macleod, 'I don't know what to say. You went after him, from what you just told me, too late. He hung on, and then suddenly, you left it too late. I guess you need to learn from it and move on.'

'You really don't get it, do you?'

Macleod thought for a moment. No, he didn't. And he was stepping into a place where he shouldn't have been .

'Let's restart this conversation. Do you want to talk to anyone else about it?' said Macleod.

'I think I will. I might give Hope a ring at home. It'll be okay to do that, won't it? I mean, it's not strictly business. It's—'

'I think she'll be quite happy to talk to you. And I think she'll appreciate I'm not the right person. I'd appreciate it if you didn't tell her how badly I messed it up.'

'Yes, of course.' Susan grabbed some of the paperwork in front of her. 'I'll get these all typed up and done.'

'Take care of yourself,' said Macleod.

It was all he could do. After all, he'd made such a mess of it. He doubted Susan would have appreciated anything more. She left the room, closed the door, and Macleod felt his heart sink a bit. It was tough to see her like that. She thought so little of herself as well. That he got. He got the fact that now, she was thinking she'd blown the chance. The big chance.

But someone like Susan would attract good people again. She'd attract all the bad sorts too, but hopefully by now she'd learnt to give them the heave-ho. Still, this was not police work. And therefore, he needed to keep a distance. He'd be available, but he was not getting into the nitty-gritty of relationship chat.

A call came down from upstairs, Tanya advising that Emmett wanted a video conference with him, and now. Macleod gave a sigh, advised Ross in the outer office what he was doing, and headed back up to his own. When he got there, Tanya was behind his desk.

'I've set it up, the link's live, all good to go,' she said.

'You didn't have to; I wasn't asking you to do that,' he said.

'No,' she said, 'Emmett asked me to do it. He said the last one was, well . . .'

'He said what?'

'He said it didn't go so well.'

'Is that what he really said?'

'We can actually hear all of this,' said a voice. It was Sabine, her voice coming from the computer's speakers.

'Right,' said Macleod, sitting down. He looked at the screen and saw Emmett, Sabine close up, and Perry in the background.

'What's happening?'

Emmett relayed the previous work they'd done regarding Heidi Schmidt, if that was her name. She seemed to be panicked about her image being taken and had potentially stolen the camera that had taken it. He also detailed Sabine's efforts and how a DC Lauren Shea was looking for Alex, and how Lauren Shea didn't exist in the police force.

'And to whom have you shown the image of her face?'

'Checked with Border Force. They don't know her,' said Emmett. 'Perry made a good point.'

'I was just saying,' said Perry from the back of the bedroom, 'that this person isn't known by Border Force, IDs aplenty, doesn't like their face to get seen, is hunting down Alex. Speaks to me of hitwoman.'

Macleod's face creased up. He'd had enough of this. He'd had enough of people hunting people down. The team had been hunted down recently. It wasn't on. He remembered the good old days of chasing people on the beat? Those early days when he walked Glasgow streets. People just ran, and you ran after them. It wasn't all this. Well, there was. He just wasn't working at that level at the time.

'I'm going to need to make a call.'

He picked up the phone and dialled a number. Macleod sat back in his seat. He knew that the other three were watching him through the video link. It took a few minutes, but then a voice came back telling him to send a request through his video link to a certain number. He didn't know the person he was talking to, but he did as he was told. Or rather, he called in Tanya and got her to do it.

When she did, Macleod was advised that someone was in the waiting room for the video link. Tanya told him to press a button when he wanted them in, but they came in anyway. A separate window opened up showing a face that everyone recognised.

'Well, good evening,' Anna Hunt said. Anna was the head of the shadowy government-backed Service, a secret agency Macleod knew too well. 'Haven't we seen enough of each other lately?'

'Sorry to bother you,' said Macleod. 'I need some information.'

'You never call me for coffee like you used to do,' said Anna. Macleod seemed to redden slightly, but he fought hard against it. The other three looked on with great interest.

'We've got a problem,' said Macleod, and asked Emmett to detail everything he'd found out. After he'd done so, Perry chipped in from the back. 'I suggested it might be a hitwoman, sounded like it to me. All the detail that was in there.'

Anna Hunt stopped for a minute, looked away to a different computer screen, and she could be heard typing something in. Her screen then went blank as somebody entered her room.

'Is she gone?' asked Emmett.

'No,' said Macleod. 'Somebody's come in to tell her something that we can't hear. She'll either be back on in a minute or two, having talked to them, or she'll be racing away from there and the call will just end.'

He sat there with a wry smile on his face. He may have been a DCI, but he still had to hang on to speak to certain people. Anna Hunt was not someone he could demand the presence of. Her image appeared again on the screen.

'Sorry,' she said, 'I had to answer something right away. I'm sure you know how it is.'

'Of course,' said Macleod, though he had no idea what it was like.

'From what you say,' said Anna, 'it would appear to me that Perry's right. I told you that man had a good sense for the Service.' In the background, Perry smiled. 'Trouble is, she's a very expensive one. I don't recognise any of the names you've said, but I recognise the method. Two rooms at a hotel, body left in the second one. She's probably sent an image of the dead man to her client, who's told her, it's not him; it's the wrong person. Or maybe they checked the DNA if they don't actually know his face. This is a clever operator, very clever. Foreign, not been caught so far, barely been traced at all. I'm going to do a little research on the side. There are rumours of a person.'

'Rumours?' said Emmett. 'Where do you get rumours?'

'Rumours, Inspector Grump, are what we call unsubstanti-ated information. This woman, we know her, we know her methods, but we have nothing to place an ID on her. Struggling with locations, struggling to know where she operates. I know that we believe she likes to travel by motorbike. That's a very strong hunch.'

'Anything else?' asked Macleod.

'No, Seoras, nothing else, and that's not because I'm with-holding it from you. Nothing else, because I have nothing else. She has operated little in the UK. I don't believe she has any confirmed kills in the UK. Although that seems to have changed just now. Be very careful. She won't hesitate to despatch the person she's looking for. And she'll not hesitate to despatch anyone who stops her from doing that.'

'Okay,' said Macleod. 'That's understood.'

'Have I given you enough?' said Anna. 'I'll come back to you. But I'm not protecting you on this one. This isn't like the last case. This is someone who I can't confirm operating here.'

She disappeared from the call, and Macleod could see Emmett's unhappy face. 'You need to say something?' asked Macleod.

'We're chasing after Alex. He's probably got a hitwoman coming after him. Just been told to watch ourselves by the head of the Service. Yes, I'm bothered. I'm very bothered. I'm running in the dark here with a lot of stuff as it is. Barely able to keep up. We don't have many people either.'

'No, we don't,' said Macleod. 'We need to find him before she finds him.'

'Well, we've gone down the line. We've checked all the places. Other than grabbing him out of the blue, which won't happen now because he'll go to ground. It's unlikely that he'll surface much. Not after the incident at the NEC. If he realises someone's dead, if he's clever enough—'

'We have all these groups,' said Macleod, 'in Birmingham. Drug recovery groups. And you have found him in one. He's been there for a while. It's clearly not where he's getting his help from. And yet, he has had help because he's got to a better state given how he's operating. So, somebody else must have turned him around. If he was at a point where he was functioning,' said Macleod, 'maybe he got help beyond that level. Those who can afford anything better go to better.'

'Are you suggesting he's got money?' said Emmett.

'Well, his family had money. His sister's clearly got money. So maybe he has some stashed away. Maybe she helped him. Who knows, maybe there's been private therapy in place.

Maybe not recently, but in the past. Maybe he's got himself to a level where he's able to use the basic services now.'

'That's a bit of a stretch,' said Emmett.

'No, it's not,' said Perry. 'It's not. Think about it. He's probably not going to want help from the family. But if he's taken it, got to a level where he can get something else. Now he'll drop them. It's not guaranteed, but it's an excellent shot. They might have an address from the past, an address from before. He will not buy fresh places all the time. So maybe he's had one. Maybe he's not drifting. Maybe he's had money to—'

'That's what I was thinking,' said Macleod. 'He's gone to ground, too. If you go to ground with other people, other druggies, you'll be able to find him. People go round, they pay money. People speak, especially when they have needs. Private therapy route. That's what you search next,' said Macleod.

'There's another thing I'm thinking of though,' said Emmett. 'Motorbike. Anna Hunt said motorbike. She likes to travel on a motorbike. I'm assuming this is the same person. She's been to the drug recovery group. She's been at the NEC. Why would you change motorbike? She will not need to change it. Nobody's suspecting her. Certainly not at that point. She thinks she's got away without her image being seen. After all, she's got the camera. She doesn't know that we know about her acting as a fake police constable. There could be a motorbike in common here in all the places.'

'Good,' said Macleod. 'It's a long shot, but it's somewhere to go and there are not a lot of places to go. Private therapy and a motorbike—what more could you want?'

Chapter 20

Emmett sat looking at various images across a multitude of screens. Most of them were images of streets centred on the drug therapy group that the fake detective had attended. Others were of the car park of the NEC and of the car park of the hotel beside it. Earlier that day, he'd gone to DCI Travers to explain what he'd been doing and what he'd found out.

Travers was cautiously interested, thought that what Emmett had going was a possibility, but there was nothing concrete yet. She thought it rather fancy when he talked about a hitwoman. But certainly, an interested detective on the outside, a game was a possibility. But she told him in no uncertain terms, she needed to find Alex Baird.

The body that was in the room at the hotel at the NEC had now been identified. It was a Carl Paxson. Carl had been attending the NEC and was a keen board gamer. However, he hadn't gone dressed in a grey hoodie, and his family didn't know where it had come from. He was a bit of a loner, which is why nobody had flagged up that Carl hadn't returned. It was only now, a few days after the event, that no one had seen him or heard of him and had contacted the police. As these processes go, eventually someone looked at the face from the hotel room and he was positively identified.

Emmett thought it was this that had led to Travers warming a little to him. Not quite jumping all over him but at least entertaining the possibility that Emmett could be correct. It certainly lent him kudos and meant he got to spend time in this room in one of the Birmingham police stations. He also had people assisting him in rounding up the footage from the CCTVs at both locations. Now he was spending the time going through it with a constable beside him, who was there more to facilitate the images rather than to study them carefully.

Emmett knew also that he was well clear of Sabine and had been for a large part of this investigation. It felt more like it used to be. If ever there was a job that required one of you to run off on your own while others stayed in pairs, Emmett was always the one sent away. Working with Sabine, there were just the two of them. Until Perry had come down, they were usually together unless single-person operations were required.

He didn't feel bad when that happened because everybody was out on their own, but when you were constantly the one being sent off, it got to you. Not that Emmett demanded a lot of company. Yes, he'd been seeing a lot of Sabine outside of work, but then she was becoming interested in what he was doing. She'd taken part in many of the board games and gaming sessions he'd gone to. Sabine was falling for it. She was gaining a love of the dice, so to speak.

Emmett had always been a loner. At school he'd seen the attractive girls, he'd seen the ones who were popular, those who were less popular, but all of them were out of reach. Very few of them ever seemed to be interested in Emmett, or what he was doing. He'd learnt not to be bothered, and yet he was a man. There was a part of him that certainly sought a female touch.

Maybe it was because of his isolation or maybe it was because of his nature, but he just didn't look at women the same way. That didn't mean he wasn't interested. He just wasn't, well, so obvious about it and so desperate. So many of the guys at school were desperate. Had to have a girlfriend. Had to be—oh there were some coarse terms going around—'Banging something.' That was probably one of the politest ones.

And then he kind of wandered into the police, and detective work because he was very analytical. He could see things. Knew what was going on. He just had to prove it. Emmett could put things together. He had an understanding of the world that came from watching it from a different viewpoint.

For instance, this bike. Anna Hunt had said that the woman liked motorbikes. She had said next to nothing else. The one thing people knew about her was that she liked the motorbike. Seemed the obvious thing to go for then, even though it was almost a throwaway comment. After all, would she not just travel by some other means? Well, no. Not if they said it she liked the bike, to be on a bike most of the time.

His time with DI Clarissa Urquhart on the Arts team had been interesting. The woman was crackers. Absolute crackers. Emmett wasn't so rude to say things about people, but he certainly thought them. And of all the people at the Inverness station, Clarissa was the most nuts. He wondered how Macleod tolerated her. But she certainly was passionate about her work. Just so erratic.

But his short time with her had brought one good thing. He'd met Sabine. Cool and calm. Quiet. Not demanding. Her coming into his world had been a good thing, a great thing. It was just, sometimes he felt, well . . . yes . . . he felt that way about her. It was hard not to. And while they were working together, that was fine. But now she was off doing something else, and part of his day was spent without her. That's how you knew, wasn't it? When they weren't there, and you were thinking about them. That's how you knew you were, well, more than just buddies, wasn't it?

'Are you ready for the next ones?' asked the constable beside him. She was blonde, in her early twenties and extremely attractive. While a pleasant enough person, Emmett was feeling nothing towards her, not even on a more basic level. Instead, she was just a colleague, just someone to work with.

Emmett stared at the screen, and then he saw in the corner a flash of red. It was a bike. It certainly was a motorbike, and it was carefully positioned away from where the CCTV camera was. The bike was almost hidden between two cars, parked unusually for a motorbike. He couldn't read the number plate from where he was, but it was definitely a red bike.

'Anne, can you keep that running?'

The blonde-haired constable beside him nodded, operated some controls, and Emmett watched as time passed by on the screen, but the bike didn't move. The car in front of it moved, and another one parked up, and then changed again until suddenly someone approached from the far end of the CCTV. You could barely see them at all. Their head was down, a baseball cap on. And they climbed on board the motorbike. It was reversed, and then sped off down the street.

'Blast it,' said Emmett. 'Can't see that number plate.'

'We may have got a view of it,' said Anne.

'How?' asked Emmett. 'I haven't seen any camera aimed in

that direction.'

'Well, we haven't gone into Bonn yet.'

'Bonn?'

'Not CCTV from the street cameras. There was a restaurant called Bonn, and the owner has a camera at the top of his window. It looks out almost from behind a curtain.'

'Could you see it from where you parked that bike?'

'It's tiny. You would struggle,' said Anne.

'Get me the footage.'

Emmett waited for a few minutes until Anne pulled another image up on the screen, and there it was in full view—the license plate of the bike. He made a note of it.

'Can we run that against the NEC license recognition? It's got a license plate recognition system coming into the car park, hasn't it?'

'Hotel certainly has,' she said. 'I think the NEC does too.'

'Run that.'

Emmett sat there staring at the image on the screen. It was definitely a woman on the bike. The shape without going to any detailed measurement looked correct—the height of the woman, the way her shoulders were, everything looked correct. She had thrown a small holdall into the pannier at the back of the bike. Maybe she'd gone and got changed from being a detective constable. He sat sipping his coffee, wondering, and then Anne came back.

'I've got a match, Inspector.'

'Emmett. Just because I'm from away doesn't mean you can't call me Emmett. It's fine.'

'We've got a match though. It's from the NEC car park, not the hotel.'

'Of course. Why would you put it into the hotel? Parked

quite a distance away, probably.'

'I don't know from this. It is one of the farthest car parks she went into. Long stay. Airport type one. I think it's if you're there for a while.'

Emmett looked at the screen. 'You need to trace that bike then,' he said. 'Go run the number plate for me.'

Anne disappeared, leaving Emmett on his own.

Got you, he thought. *I got you. Now how to find you.*

* * *

'You do it this time,' said Sabine.

'I'm merely here to assist,' said Perry. 'This is your gig, you take the lead. You wouldn't take the lead over Emmett, would you?'

'My gig, is it? You're sent down to assist. And besides, I'm Sergeant Ferguson, you're a constable.'

'No, you're not using that one. Macleod wouldn't have let Hope take off first. He was the one to ask the questions. No one else. You're not doing that to me. I bet you Emmett goes in and asks the questions first before you.'

'No, he doesn't actually,' said Sabine. 'Emmett can be quite quiet. He actually likes his colleague to jump in first. He sits back and assesses.'

'Is that with every colleague?' Sabine looked at Perry. 'What? It's a straightforward enough question.'

'Well, I don't know,' said Sabine. 'I worked with him when he was with Clarissa and the arts team, but he knew nothing about the arts. So I asked the questions first, because, well, in that gig you have to know a bit of what you're about.'

'And before that?'

'Before that, he was, well, I thought he was in Glasgow, wasn't he? You'd have known him from then.'

'He was on his own most of the time then. At least from what I remember,' said Perry. 'I was wondering if he'd make it. He was ostracised by many people.' Sabine looked at him, almost fiercely.

'Well, not by me. I didn't know him. Big place, I had my own issues. No, the way you looked at me there, well . . .'

'Well, what?'

'No, I'm out,' said Perry. 'Too much going on at the moment, anyway.'

'Too much what?' said Sabine.

'You go first,' said Perry, 'and I'll tell you afterwards.'

Sabine shook her head as the pair walked up and into the offices of yet another drug recovery specialist. This one had a secretary, along with lots of qualifications on the wall. Sabine looked at them and was impressed. They had called ahead, and now they got to enter the offices of a rather older woman. She was maybe sixty-five or beyond and had a very serious demeanour.

'I'm not at liberty to give out any details about my client,' said the woman.

'Your client may be in trouble. We're trying to track him at the moment. There's a consensus that someone may try to kill him. We want to get to him first.'

'You're telling me his life's at stake?'

'Yes,' said Sabine.

'I haven't seen or heard of Alex for over a year now. No, eighteen months. He did some good work, seemed to be getting better and then he quit. Left.'

'Did he talk about anyone special while he was here?' asked

169

Sabine.

'I don't see that's relevant to finding him.'

'There was a woman called Precious. Was there anybody beyond that?'

'Now, he spoke of Precious. He was fond of her. Very fond of her. Was visiting her.'

'But no one else?'

'No one else,' said the older woman.

'We don't believe he had any other romantic attachments, if you can put it that way,' said Sabine. 'Are you aware of any others?'

'No.'

'Do you have an address for him?'

'We have an address,' said the woman. 'I don't know how current it is. Like I said, I haven't seen him in eighteen months.'

'But you had at least seen him. He was on your books, so to speak.'

'He was. And he paid by cash.'

'Cash?' said Sabine.

'I believe he was getting money from a family. He didn't want me to know the family. Yes, he told me first names when we were discussing it. But he didn't want me to have the ability to reach out to them or for them to reach to me. So, I believe they sent the money, and he brought it to me for his sessions.'

'Unusual,' said Sabine.

'It is. I did check. I did make sure it wasn't coming from things like drug sales or money being laundered or anything like that. He was a soul who needed help. And I helped him.'

'Can we get that address?' asked Sabine.

The woman reached into a drawer, pulled out an envelope and handed it over. 'That's his address. I'm giving you this because you're saying his life is in danger. If it's not—'

'It is,' said Perry. 'It is, and we have been searching everywhere to find some way of getting hold of him. This is a long shot but thank you.'

Sabine wondered what it was about Perry. People just seemed to be happy when he gave an answer to something. Was it the inflection in the voice? Was it the jovial face? Was it the dishevelled look that did it? What was it about Perry that people eventually warmed to him? Some people warmed immediately.

They came out, opened up the envelope, and read an address. It was a Birmingham address, and Sabine plugged it into her phone.

'Other side of the city from us,' said Sabine.

'Well, that makes sense. You don't want to be going around the corner if you're trying to keep people away from you. If they find out where you go to get your head sorted, then maybe they'll think you live nearby. Obviously, he came to someone who was well away.'

'That's close to where Emmett was working out of today, though, wasn't it?'

'Yes,' said Perry. 'That's where Emmett is. Not around the corner, but what, ten minutes?'

'It'll take us a good forty minutes plus to get across town. Maybe we send him.'

'Ask him to go,' said Perry.

'Ask him to go?'

'I don't send anybody. I'm not of a high enough rank to send people, but if I were a sergeant, I certainly wouldn't be sending my inspector.'

'What?' said Sabine, for Perry was looking at her and

smirking.

'Just be careful how you make it work.'

'What are you on about?' said Sabine. She raised her hand to her hair, brushing it out behind her. It was done almost subconsciously.

'He's a decent guy. I hope you can make it work.'

Sabine ignored him. 'I'd better phone him,' said Sabine, 'to get him there.'

'Do you want me to do it? You look a little red,' said Perry. Sabine threw a punch, hitting Perry gently on the shoulder.

* * *

Sabine called Emmett, who immediately jumped at the chance to race round to the address of Alex Baird. He also told her in an excitable fashion about the red bike he'd discovered. Sabine and Perry tried to make their way across the city through the traffic of the day. Some cities functioned well, but even in those, progress was usually slow. Birmingham was very slow. It took almost an hour before they arrived. When they got there, Sabine stepped out of the car. Perry shouted after, 'Where are you going?'

'I've got to follow him in.'

'You don't know what he's met in there. You haven't heard from him. Emmett could be in deep conversation. You could spook the guy. The guy could run. Probably wiser just to hang fire. Or even phone him at first. Message him. See if he wants us to follow in.'

'You're probably right,' said Sabine. She got back inside the car. At which point, Perry opened his passenger door and jumped out.

'What the hell?' said Sabine. Perry looked back quickly and pointed his hand down the street.

'Red bike!' he shouted. 'Red bike.'

Chapter 21

Emmett had approached the house given to Sabine by the therapist. The street was like so many in the city. Crowded, with cars everywhere fighting for a parking space. And yet, the houses looked so drab.

There was a small patch at the front of the house, meant to be a front lawn. But in truth, it was just a mess of rubbish and stones. The door had paint peeling off it. The window beside the door was boarded up. There was a tile or two missing off the roof, and there were possibly more absent, but Emmett couldn't see that high from his current position.

He approached the door, looked for a bell, but there was none. There wasn't even a knocker. So, he rapped on the door with his hand. It took a while before he heard movement, so he rapped again. The house was in a row of terraced houses. However, there was an entry down between this one and the next one, and Emmett decided, when the door wasn't opened, that he should walk down the entry.

When he reached the rear, he found a yard at the back of the house, which was as much of a tip as the front garden. The back door, however, seemed to be of a weaker construction. He approached it and found that it swung open with no lock on it.

Emmett stepped inside and then listened. He could hear snoring. Slowly, he walked around the ground floor of the house. There was a living room at the front where the window was boarded up. There was an old TV, a sofa that was so worn it was unbelievable. Beer cans and bottles lay about the place, and he saw the remains of little white packets of powder. Clearly, whoever it was, hadn't got over something.

He crept his way up the stairs, following the snoring. Turning left at the top, Emmett opened the door from which the snoring was coming. There was no furniture in the room. Instead, there was a suitcase at the far end, into which some clothes were dumped. Lying on the floor, on what looked like a mat, was a man, the source of the snoring.

Emmett looked at the photograph on his phone of a younger Alex Baird. It could be. Rather than wake him, he searched the rest of the top floor and found nothing. There was a bathroom that had mould across the walls. Another room had cockroaches running up and down. Emmett returned to the bedroom. He reached down and tapped the man on the side.

There was nothing. Hardly any movement at all. If it weren't for the rise and fall of the man's chest and the loud snoring, Emmett might have thought he was dead. Emmett, this time, kicked him gently with his foot.

'Meh,' said the man. And then his eyes opened. He seemed to struggle to focus. Emmett stood over him.

'Ugh,' said the man. And suddenly he was backing himself into a corner. He was clearly looking around for something. A weapon, possibly. So, Emmett reached into his coat and pulled out his warrant card.

'DCI Emmett Grump. You have nothing to fear from me. I realise someone may be after you, but that someone is not me. Are you Alex Baird?'

The man nodded. Emmett opened his coat up and patted himself down, showing there were no weapons.

'I'm investigating the death of your father, Martin Baird. I believe it may have something to do with a game called Majik Falls.'

'Never heard of Majik Falls.'

'Rubbish,' said Emmett. 'Absolute rubbish. You know Majik Falls as well as I do. You're a gamer. I know that from Precious.'

'I need to get cleaned up,' said the man.

'Are you back on them? The drugs? I had hoped you might have got off them.'

'Bit of a shock recently. Death of a friend.'

'Friend or just someone you bumped into? Someone you swapped your top with. I was there at the NEC, you see,' said Emmett. 'We were the ones trying to get to you before somebody else got to you.'

'They killed him, didn't they?'

'How did you know him?' asked Emmett.

'Didn't,' said Alex. 'I swapped my top with him. He said to me, "I haven't got that one." I was being chased. So I swapped and got out of there.'

'You went to see Orla. Orla Jones.'

'Yes,' he said.

'Why? Was it to do with the game? Was it to do with what happened with the game?'

'I don't need a reason to see Orla. Orla's just . . .' The man seemed to drift away for a moment.

'But Majik Falls? Is that not why you're here? Is that not why you're hiding? Someone coming after you because of Majik Falls? Did Orla come after you? Has Orla sent this person?'

'Orla wouldn't send anyone. Orla was . . . Orla's lovely. Orla's just . . .'

'Orla's high up in Samson Games,' said Emmett. 'You know that's a—'

'Subsidiary of Whirl Pit. Yes. Made it big, all of them, didn't they? Made it big.'

'Tell me where you know all of them from. And who they all are.'

'I need to straighten out,' said the man. Alex tried to stand up. He stumbled for a bit. 'I get a shower. I get a shower and then.'

'We can give you a shower. We'll go down to the station. Be safer.'

'No, no. I need to go here.'

He stood up, and Emmett realised that the man only had pants on and a t-shirt.

'I'll tell you what you want,' said Alex. 'I need to do this first. It's just the bathroom. There's nowhere to go. You've been in, probably, have you? Can't get out the window. You can sit outside the door, it's fine.'

Emmett nodded and watched as the man half-stumbled his way out of the room and over to the bathroom. The door closed, and Emmett walked downstairs. He took up a vantage point at the front, where the small bathroom window was. It was true; getting out from the top floor would be difficult and obvious. Nonetheless, Emmett covered the possibility.

Alex was forty minutes in the shower, and Emmett thought he must have been some sort of teenager. Biding his time, Emmett looked around the building. Here and there were photographs of die-cast metal figures that were a staple of the gaming community. All those models associated with various games. Why were there photographs of them?

Emmett looked closer. They were ripped out of magazines. Was this a way of fuelling his love for gaming? Did he go into the newsagent's and rip out the pictures? Did he grab the magazine, run off with it and then do it?

Emmett wondered what sort of life this guy had. He looked terrible when he was going for a shower. The hair was tousled. It was longer than it should have been. His eyebrows had grown. Again, not trimmed. Not looked after. He clocked the nails that were long. The man was a mess.

Alex came downstairs after his shower, insisted on putting the kettle on, and then offered Emmett a coffee. Emmett looked at it. It came from a packet. Maybe he'd lifted them from somewhere. Emmett wasn't sure, but he politely took the coffee, though he watched what went into it. A large shot of whiskey went into Alex's, but Emmett refused when he was offered the same.

Almost an hour had gone since Emmett had walked in, but finally he would get to hear from Alex. He settled himself down in what was a deck chair while Alex lay on the deeply abused sofa.

'Tell me. Tell me about it all. I want to know about your father. Why your father was in Mellon-Udrigle.'

'Nobody knows.'

'Do you know we found something recently? We found two dice. The mage's dice. Handmade ones in Mellon-Udrigle. Close to where your father was decapitated. He died not long after Majik Falls was starting to do well. How well do you know Majik Falls?' asked Emmett.

'Intimately,' said Alex and smiled. 'I know it intimately.'

'Were you behind it?'

Alex grinned. And then he turned away. Emmett could feel his phone vibrating. He reached into his pocket, took it out, and saw a message from Sabine. It said, 'Hit woman here. Get out.'

Emmett jumped up. 'You need to go,' he said.

Alex was stunned. 'I need to what?' But Emmett was already grabbing him by the arm.

'You need to go.' He could hear the back door suddenly open. There were two ways into the living room from the back door. You could come down the main hall and into the front living room, or you could cut through what was a rather small dining room and in through another door.

'You go to the front door,' said Emmett. 'I'll see who's coming through.'

Emmett pushed him across the living room and then burst into the dining room. As he did so, he saw a woman walking in. Then Emmett pulled himself back as she was making for the main hall. He looked around him. There was an iron bar lying up against the wall.

He realised from the bottom end of it the bar had been poked into some sort of fire. There was a fireplace in the living room. *Is that what Alex used to stoke it? What did it matter?*

Emmett picked it up, stepped into the dining room, and from a distance flung the iron bar. The woman who had entered had no time to react, and the bar clattered into her, hard and heavy, knocking her to the floor. A gun she was carrying fell, and Emmett ran across the dining room and slid under a breakfast bar to where the gun was.

He threw the gun away. Emmett then felt a blow, hard into

179

the back of his neck. For a moment, everything went black, and then everything was bright again, but the back of his neck was screaming. He could hear the footsteps moving away from the kitchen, moving away from him, and a cry outside.

* * *

'Let's hope he gets it,' said Sabine, as she approached the front door. It burst open, and a man ran out. He reared up for a moment, until Sabine yelled, 'Police!' at him. He turned, pointing behind him. 'She's coming, she's coming.'

'Behind me,' said Sabine. She stepped forward, allowing the man to get behind her, and then saw the approach of a woman. The woman was trim, muscular to a degree, and Sabine squared up to fight. If she could get up close to the door, the woman couldn't get around her. Sabine stepped quickly towards it.

The woman realised that too, and as they came quickly together, they met just under the lintel of the door. Sabine fired a punch that was ducked under by the other woman, who grabbed Sabine and twisted her arm. Sabine let out a yell, but kicked hard down, hitting the woman in the knees.

The grip was freed for a moment, and Sabine pulled back. The woman tried to push past, but Sabine caught her, lifting a knee up. It was more of a block than a strike, and the woman turned to engage with Sabine. She placed a hand on her neck, and the next second, she was being throttled on the ground. A hand choking the life out of her. Sabine's eyes watered. But from behind her, she could see another figure approaching.

Perry pulled out a nightstick. Seeing Sabine on the floor, he'd raced in. The woman who was choking Sabine clearly hadn't clocked he was coming, and he hit her hard across the face. The woman let go of Sabine, reached up and hit Perry hard right on the chin. Perry stepped backwards two, three, four times then hit the small wall at the edge of the garden. He was moving backwards so fast that instead of just falling down, he fell over the wall and landed on his front.

He rolled up as best he could, but already the woman was out on the street running. The man who had come out, however, was further down the street and jumping on a bus. The woman ran hard, waving at the bus, but as it pulled off, disappearing into the Birmingham evening, the woman looked around for a moment. Then the woman ran back towards them.

She went over towards the motorbike Perry had previously spotted, leaving Perry sprawling on the floor. Sabine was now up on her feet.

'Stop her,' she shouted. 'Perry, stop her.' The woman kicked down, opened the throttle on the bike, and went to start it. There was a splutter, then nothing. Again, a splutter, then nothing. Once more, a splutter, then nothing. The woman dropped the bike and ran off across the street in the opposite direction from the bus. Sabine went to go after her but the pain meant she couldn't even get going. Perry was flat out, staring at the woman as she left.

From his prone position, Perry pulled out his phone and dialled into the nearest station. Sabine could hear him calling in the situation. She turned toward the house. Where was Emmett?

The woman had been brutal. Sabine knew how to fight, but this woman . . . This woman was like going up against Kirsten. This woman was something else. For a moment, her heart sank. *Emmett*, she thought. *Emmett*.

She stumbled towards the front door. Hearing a moan from the rear, Sabine ran down the hall. In the kitchen, she couldn't see anyone, but then there was another murmur. She bent down, looking under the breakfast bar. He was lying there, clearly sore, but he was alive. She slid down beside him, taking his face in her hands.

'Thank God,' she said. 'You're okay. You're okay.' Before he could answer, she planted a deep kiss on his lips. 'Oh, thank God, Emmett,' she said, throwing her arms around him.

Chapter 22

'We were so close,' said Sabine.

'He's still alive, though,' said Emmett. 'Thanks to you two spotting the bike.'

'You were the one who thought of it first,' said Sabine. 'We got lucky, though. Anna Hunt was right. She was a professional. I didn't stand a chance, going toe to toe. I'd have been dead except for Perry here.'

'Perry here is quite sore.' Sabine looked at Perry. She wanted to give him a hug, but he pushed her back.

'Don't,' he said. 'I think the ribs are bruised.'

'Are you okay? No?' asked Emmett.

'There's nothing broken, I think, just a bit of bruising. My jaw feels like it's been hit by a brick wall. Nothing I won't come back from,' said Perry. 'But don't tell Tanya, okay? We don't need any big-hero stories. She'll just worry.'

'Where do we go from here, though?' asked Sabine. 'Alex is gone; he's not coming back here. Not when he knows she knows where he lives. And she's at large too. She'll be hunting him down.'

'Well, we don't know where he's going. We did well to find this place. But imagine the next place he goes to. Nobody will know where it is. At least he's got half a brain on him,' said Emmett. 'Well, I think he does.'

'He could still come for drugs, though,' said Sabine.

'Doubt it. It's going to be a long haul. It's going to be difficult to find him. No, I don't think we'll find him by sending out a wide net anymore. But we have this,' said Emmett, pointing to the building he'd just come out of.

'Well, he lived there,' said Perry. 'I guess there could be something.'

'Did he say much to you, though, about what's really going on, about his place in it?' asked Sabine.

'He went for a shower. I was trying not to spook him,' said Emmett. 'When he came down to sit to talk to me, well, that's when she came in.'

'Then that's all we've got,' said Perry, looking at the house. 'Guess it's time to glove up and search.'

A car pulled up, and DCI Travers got out. 'Causing a bit of a stir,' she said.

'I found Alex Baird. He's deeply involved in this . . . though I'm not totally sure how.'

'But you found him. Where is he now?' asked Travers.

'I think my idea of a hitwoman was accurate. She came. We were lucky to get out alive. Alex jumped on a bus.'

'Then we'll need to search the footage. Find out where he's gone.'

'We can do,' said Emmett. 'I think he'll disappear, though. Back underground. He'll soon be gone.'

'Nonetheless, it's what we'll do.'

'We do have here,' said Emmett. 'We can search in here.'

'It's a bit of a drug house, isn't it? What are you hoping to find?' asked Travers.

'I don't know,' said Emmett. 'I'm going to take Sabine and Perry here to search the place.'

'Careful with it,' said Travers. 'And tell me what you find, okay? I'll get onto this bus. Get a sergeant down here, too. Run things for me. You can tell him the times of what happened. I'll pull through on that side, okay? You check the house out.'

Travers gave Emmett a nod, and he realised that this was her saying, 'You were right.' But that was all that was going to be said. Emmett took it in good grace and then told Sabine and Perry to follow him inside the house.

'I'll take upstairs,' said Emmett. 'You start downstairs, Sabine. Perry, you see if there's anything under the stairs or around the edges of the house. Anything hidden under the rubbish in the garden or yard.'

'Thanks,' said Perry. 'Garden's an absolute tip.'

'Good man,' said Emmett. Emmett made his way up the stairs and then into the first bedroom. There was next to nothing there, as Emmett had already noted. But now, he felt around the floorboards. It wasn't long before he found one that came up. He reached underneath, and there was a plastic bag. He pulled at it and soon he had the item in his grasp.

Bringing it out and setting it down on the floorboards, he realised it was a 1973 edition of Whippet Races, an early board game, but an important one. He turned it over inside the bag, and then he carefully unzipped the ziplock it was in. While wearing gloves, he removed the board game and lifted it up.

It was the first edition. It had the die-cast characters, not the plastic ones that came in the later editions. Carefully, he replaced the items in the box and put the box back in the ziplock. He then reached back down into the hole he'd removed the game from. With his arm all the way in, he found another ziplock bag. He took this out and found a small box of cards. They were contained in a white cardboard box with no words on the outside. Carefully, he opened the box and saw the cards inside. He lifted out the first one, turning it over in his hands.

'Firelands,' he blurted. 'Firelands. This is the prototype of Firelands. This would be worth a fortune.'

He took out the next card, and the one after that, and the one after that. He fell down on his backside, going through all the cards. This was the prototype of Firelands. Emmett had a first edition in his house. But this, this made the first edition look like nothing.

One of the cards had writing on it in pencil. Studying the card, he realised it was different to the first edition card, and written in pencil was the change that was made. For a moment, Emmett held it up for examination. Then he heard a slight knock on the open bedroom door.

'Am I disturbing you, or would you like to be left alone with your game?' Emmett turned his head and Sabine was standing there holding a game wrapped up in a ziplock bag.

'Don't crush that!' said Emmett suddenly.

'Why?' said Sabine. 'It's just a board game.'

'That's not just a board game; that's a 1995 edition of something that didn't really take. New Man. That's a New Man game.'

'And?'

'Run of five hundred only, except that's from the first fifty. The ones they put out, sent out to people who had helped them. They'll be signed.'

Sabine flipped it over, looked at the back, and saw the signature.

'What's it worth?' asked Sabine.

'That's priceless.'

'Yeah, I get it; it's a really important game. But what's it worth?' asked Sabine.

'That'll be a grand at the most, but anybody that collects, they'd break somebody's arm off for that.'

'I never really thought that was a side of you,' said Sabine.

'I've found two others. I think there's more.'

Sabine nodded, advised she would search some more downstairs but left the New Man game up with Emmett. Gradually, as they combed the house, more and more games appeared. The collection was about forty strong by the time they'd finished, all hidden away, all in places that people wouldn't go. Perry even found one out in the rear garden in a little wooden box.

'He was a true collector,' said Emmett. 'This stuff here, it makes my collection just look—'

'Rubbish,' suggested Perry.

'A little less than fabulous,' said Emmett, glaring at Perry.

'Do you think he'll come back for it?' asked Perry.

'Maybe,' said Emmett, 'but he's just been threatened. He might think that this will all sit here, and we certainly don't want to be advising anyone that we've got it. Not out to the press.'

Emmett looked through all the games. Perry was struggling to understand the excitement. After all, they were just in ziplock bags. What was the importance of them? They were Alex's treasure.

Sabine watched Emmett. A little glow of pride inside her because she could see the love he had for the games. He was in his element with them.

'Hang on a minute,' said Emmett. He had before him a card game. The box said, 'Fiesta.' The brightly coloured cards were all sitting in front of him. However, one card looked slightly dimmer. It wasn't as thick and could crease up more.

'What's that?' asked Sabine.

'There was a print and play set that came with this, done recently, in the last five years.'

'Print and play set? What are those?' asked Perry.

'You'd have the original game, and some people would release expansions that would go with the game. However, some were doing them online, so you could just print them off and make up your own cards from them. Now, obviously, they wouldn't be as good, but some people got it down to a fine art. These aren't. These are just printed off, which I find strange in this collection. I think this was an expansion. I think you could buy the actual physical expansion, as well as print and play it.'

'And that surprises you because?' asked Sabine.

'The edition. Look how good it is. Fiesta. This is an original Fiesta. You don't put print and play cards with it. And besides,' he said, as he flicked through the print and play cards, 'this one's wrong.'

'How do you know this?' asked Perry.

Emmett turned slowly and looked at Perry. 'Some people know their cars,' he said. 'Some people know their celebrities. Some people will tell you about aircraft. They'll tell you about dishwashers. They'll tell you about family trees, great engineering feats. This is my world, Perry. This is my world.'

'But what's up with it?' asked Sabine.

'This card's wrong. It's just wrong; it shouldn't be in here.'

'It looks the same as all the rest though,' said Perry. 'Are you sure?'

Emmett glared at him. 'I'm telling you, this shouldn't be here. There is no edition with this one.'

He held it up in front of him, and turned the card over and over.

'What's it say?'

'It's about chasing a location; except this one's got a grid reference on it.'

'A grid reference? Are there any grids in the game?' asked Perry.

'No,' said Emmett.

'Read it out,' said Sabine, taking up her phone. She switched it to her mapping function. Emmett read out the grid reference.

'That's a forest near Inverness.'

'Near Inverness,' said Emmett. 'That's where he's from originally. Why? Why would you have a grid reference like this? Why would you put it on a card?' 'You've got it on a card,' he said, suddenly answering his own question. 'So nobody else knows about it. But you've had to write it down. You're not going to retain it in your memory. So, you put it somewhere you're not going to lose it. Somewhere innocuous. Somewhere that anybody who hasn't got a clue about games won't even bat an eye at. This is something important to Alex.'

'It's in Inverness,' said Sabine. 'It'll take us a while to get up there.'

'Can't go there yet, especially as we don't know what it is. We'll ask the big boss.' Emmett pulled out his phone and dialled a number.

* * *

Macleod stood watching Susan Cunningham and a couple of constables. They had spades with them, and although he'd offered to help, Susan wouldn't hear of it. 'Sometimes you make me feel like an old man,' he'd said. She had said that, as the senior officer, he should be available to answer questions and any phone calls that came in, and to be the first to tell Emmett what they'd found. She would put in the hard work along with the constables.

Macleod didn't feel that was right. She was a woman after all. He should take on the physical work. And then he thought about what Jane, his partner, would say to him. 'Don't be so ridiculous. We're not weaklings.'

Trouble was, it was bred into him. It's what you did back in his day. Any hard physical labour and especially digging, which was a man's job back then. You did it for the woman, whoever she was. Back then, it wasn't sexist. It was polite. Nowadays, everybody called out whatever you did, this, that or whatever. He'd just have to get on with it.

He'd agreed and, about halfway through the dig, had disappeared off to come back with some drinks. The day was not sunny, but it was warm, and Susan was digging in her jeans and had her blouse off with just a t-shirt underneath. After a few hours she was covered in soil from the knee down, but they'd gone down a couple of feet. That was when they heard the ding of a spade against something metal.

'Careful now,' said Macleod. 'Careful.'

Susan and the constables traced out where the metal stopped and then dug around it. Eventually they got down far enough to see it was a box. Slowly, they uncovered it and then lifted it out. Macleod took some photographs and then he looked to open it, but there was a lock on it.

'We'll take it to the station. I'll call Emmett.'

At the station, Macleod got the constables to take the box up to his office. Susan came up as well, and a locksmith arrived, opening the key lock without a problem. Macleod set back the lid of the box.

'It's just a game,' said Macleod, looking inside. 'There's dice here, cards. It's just a game.'

Susan looked at it. 'It doesn't say what game, though.' Macleod took a photograph, and he sent the image down to Emmett. A few minutes later, there came back another message.

Don't touch it. I'm on my way.

Chapter 23

It was two in the morning, but Macleod was still in his office. On his desk sat the box. He had removed nothing from it. He hadn't gone poking either. Sitting across from him was Susan Cunningham. He had told her to go home, but she wouldn't leave him. Instead, she had floated around, kept coming back into the office, had gone out and got Macleod food. Macleod hadn't wanted to leave the box unattended.

The two of them were now sitting in the office together, drinking coffee. The number of cups they'd already drunk had long fallen away from their memory. But now, they were getting excited. Emmett had messaged. He was only twenty minutes out. These twenty minutes seemed to take forever, but when Emmett arrived at the door of Macleod's office, knocking politely, Susan Cunningham sat up quickly.

'Come in,' said Macleod. Emmett entered, and without saying a word, walked straight over to the box on Macleod's desk. Sabine followed him.

'Normally we get some polite words of hello,' said Macleod. Then he turned to Susan. 'Get a coffee for the pair of them. I'm sure they'll be tired after driving.'

'Tired driving? I drove the whole way,' said Sabine. 'He's

been sleeping.'

Emmett ignored her. Pulling on some gloves, he looked at Macleod's table. Then he lifted the box and moved it across to a different table in the corner. He started to take all the items that were on that table and move them over to Macleod's desk.

'That's just the paperwork that Tanya's organised for me. All in a specific pile so I can sign it.'

'You've been here for how many hours? When are you going to sign it?' blurted Emmett suddenly.

'I'm the DCI. You don't get to ask the DCI questions like that. All I'm saying is that Tanya's going to be having a word with you tomorrow.'

Emmett ignored him. Running back over to the table, he lifted items out of the box. Macleod got up out of his chair. Together with Sabine, he stood back watching Emmett.

There were photos being removed. Dice. Cards. Different illustrations. Macleod went over to look at the photographs. He could see a young woman in one. And then there was a game. People playing it. Several figures around it. People holding up cards being photographed. The young woman was in lots of the photographs, and she was often seen hugging a much younger boy. The boy could only have been in his very early teens, whereas she looked like a teenager who'd just become a woman. Eighteen, nineteen, maybe something like that. Macleod went to speak, but Emmett turned around and put his hand up.

'Working on it,' he said. 'Working on it. Everyone shush.' Macleod looked at Sabine, and she just shrugged her shoulders. Gradually, in front of them on the table, they could see a pattern. Items were being laid out, dice were being put in specific areas until eventually Macleod could recognise that there were four distinct places. Four groups of cards that looked similar yet were very different. Four groups of dice, one in each, again similar but different. Emmett was examining the markings on each of these. Then he was flipping cards over, laying them out into different decks, placing some out in strange patterns.

'What have we got here?' asked Macleod.

'Don't you recognise it?' said Emmett.

'No,' said Macleod. 'Funny enough, I'm not that big on games.'

Emmett looked towards Sabine, who stood looking down at the table. Then she turned to look at Emmett. 'Similar to some of the cards we saw over in Aberdeen when we started out. Is this Majik Falls?' asked Sabine.

'Bingo,' said Emmett. 'Only this isn't just Majik Falls. This, I believe to be a prototype of Majik Falls. You're looking at history. You're looking at the creation of something that gave our generation one of the greatest games we've ever played. This is . . . this is like finding the Ark.'

'Whoa,' said Macleod. 'I think we've gone a bit overboard with the Ark.'

'Not for a gamer,' said Sabine. Susan Cunningham entered. She went to put a cup of coffee down on the table, but Emmett quickly waved her away.

'No, no. You can't touch this. We need to get this all bagged up correctly when we put it back.'

'So you're saying this is Majik Falls?' said Macleod. 'Is it in any way different?'

'Some minor differences, but very minor,' said Emmett. 'If you knew how to play Majik Falls, you could play it with this one. Not a problem. Except for one thing.'

'What?' asked Macleod.

'There's no mage dice. If you're playing the mage, you can't play. The mage dice are missing.'

'You mean the dice we found on Martin Baird? Is that what you're talking about? Do they fit here?' asked Macleod.

'They do, don't they?' said Sabine. 'This is like . . .'

'I'm sorry?' said Susan. 'This is like what?'

'This is the puzzle right in front of us. Alex had Majik Falls,' said Emmett. 'Alex. Alex is the creator.'

'You can't say that,' said Macleod. 'He's got the prototype. It doesn't make him the creator. It doesn't mean he owned it.'

'No,' said Emmett, 'not from this, but Martin Baird had those two dice. Where did he get them? Now it turns out his son has the actual game they came from.'

'Maybe he went and got it,' said Macleod.

'No,' said Emmett, 'look, the photographs, this isn't just a prototype, this is telling a story. We've got photographs here.'

Sabine studied them. 'The young lad, the twelve-year-old—you don't think that's . . .'

'Yes,' said Emmett, 'that's Alex, that's Alex, the young Alex, isn't it?'

'It could be,' said Macleod. 'We'll have to get somebody to ID that properly.'

'But there's also a young woman there,' said Sabine. 'And she's in a lot of them. And she's hugging him. She's hugging him in many of these photographs.'

'Romantically?' asked Macleod.

'No. Not quite like that. But then again, I'm not sure the boy's caring. He seems quite happy. Very happy about it.'

'He's also young for her, isn't he?' said Susan. 'I mean, even for back then. Somebody in their late teens. Somebody just getting into their teens. They're not going to be intimate or anything like that.'

'No, but they look like good buddies,' said Macleod. 'And remember, he's a teen lad. Just coming into bloom, as they say.'

The team looked at Macleod.

'Well, that's what they used to say. He's just become a proper lad, a man. He's going to start noticing women, and especially teenage women around him. I mean, look at her. She's good looking. They'll notice her, won't they? I'm sure he's delighted to be being hugged by her.'

The team looked at him once again.

'Phone Perry. Perry, Perry'll back me up on this. Where is Perry, anyway?'

'Left him down there. DCI Travers is still working out where Alex is. I thought I should leave Perry to help her.'

'Fair enough,' said Macleod. 'But you phone Perry. Perry'll back me up on this.' He turned to Emmett. 'You never felt like that.'

'I was too busy then,' he said, 'painting miniatures, playing games.'

There was a sudden silence, almost like everyone taking a breath. Then Macleod stepped forward again to look at the photographs. 'Does anybody know who this guy is? He seems to be heavily involved in the game. Seems to be bigger than most of the others. Who's he? What's he doing?'

'Is that a young Steve Dingle?' asked Sabine.

'Steve Dingle? That's the guy in charge, isn't it? Of Samson Games,' said Macleod.

'And the woman,' said Sabine. 'Orla? Is that Orla Jones?'

'It makes sense, doesn't it?' said Emmett. 'Alex has gone to meet Orla Jones, who came to the NEC. You might be on to something,' Emmett said to Macleod. 'Maybe the infatuation never stopped.'

'They say your first love's your strongest,' said Susan.

'So,' said Macleod, 'he's part of the team producing the game. Then his father is murdered. Head cut off. Dice hidden away. Why?'

'Could it be,' said Susan, 'that he's like the junior? He's the young one, and they're trying to push him out? Maybe they don't want to make it his idea? Maybe . . .'

'Maybe he's the one who came up with it,' said Emmett. 'If you all did it and you brought it to market, are you going to seriously push everybody else out of the way? It'll be your development team. But the idea comes from a young lad, and if you were ambitious enough . . .'

'But then his father comes and complains when things are on the move. Does Alex tell his dad?' asked Macleod.

'Martin Baird,' said Sabine, 'as we all know, tried to deal with things for his family and things weren't right, and he did it quietly. But he did it.'

'And somebody killed him, but he hid the dice beforehand because they had the prototype,' said Emmett.

'They must have built something else to replace it,' said Macleod.

'There was a prototype of Majik Falls. There are always prototypes. They're always building them in formal production,' said Emmett. 'But this predates that prototype. Isn't that what it is? This shows that it was made by somebody else first. He may have been in the group, or was he just hanging about with them and he made the prototype off his own bat? Is he a board-game maker?'

Sabine had gone silent, but she was looking at a photograph

that Emmett had placed at the far end of the table. It was potentially Steve Dingle, but Sabine was looking beyond Steve Dingle. Behind him, there was a woman dressed in a ninja costume. The mask was pulled up, and the long hair, as well as the face, said to Sabine that this was Orla Jones. She was holding a sword in her hand.

'I think we want to look at this.'

Macleod took it in his hand. 'And?' he said.

'That's the girl. That's the one we think is Orla Jones. She's got a sword. He was decapitated with something very sharp. Can you decapitate someone with a sword like that?'

Macleod shook his shoulders. He had no idea. Emmett took hold of it. But then Susan Cunningham grabbed the photo. She stared at it.

'That's a ninto. That's a ninja sword. Ninja swords are there for quick strikes. You don't butcher somebody as a ninja. You despatch them quickly. Quick strokes. That would take the head off anyone. If you knew how to use it, I guess. Properly.'

'Orla Jones was often in the vicinity of Mellon Udrigle, wasn't she?' said Macleod. 'Said that herself. I thought I read it in one of your reports.'

'It's true. She told us she was shocked by the news story because it was close to where she was,' said Emmett.

'What if she called Martin Baird then?' said Sabine. 'To meet. Meet there. Away from everyone. Killed him.'

'And what, Alex is coming back now? To expose her? To show what she did? Is that it?' asked Macleod. 'Where does Orla Jones live?'

'I think she's got a Glasgow address,' said Emmett. 'But . . .'

'Then I think we need to lift her,' said Macleod. 'We need to bring her in for questioning. Possibly Steve Dingle too.'

'Oh, we need to do it right then,' said Emmett. 'She'll come in with the lawyer, no doubt. We could get some sleep and then go get her.'

'No,' said Macleod. 'Get the cars. We'll go do it now.'

'It's a four-hour drive,' said Sabine.

'It is,' said Macleod. 'But luckily, Susan here isn't tired.'

Susan looked at him. 'I never said that.'

'We need to go, though. We need to go because we have got a hitwoman out there. If we can find this, if we can find Alex beforehand, or even if Orla is the one behind the hitwoman, at least we can get it stopped before the contract's carried out. It may look like we've got time, but every moment we don't go, don't get to the bottom of this, Alex is at risk.'

'We go then,' said Emmett. 'I'll pack the game up.'

'No, you won't,' said Macleod. 'I'll lock the office. I'll phone Tanya. Tanya can come in and bag this stuff, get forensics all over it. It is after all priceless, by what you say.' Emmett nodded back at him. 'Good. Anyway, let's go. It's time to get to the bottom of what happened out there.'

Chapter 24

The drive down to Glasgow seemed to take an age. In truth, it was only four hours, but it was done through the night, and Macleod couldn't sleep. Neither could Emmett behind him in the rear seat, but Sabine laid her head on Emmett's shoulder. Susan Cunningham talked to Macleod for most of the drive. Usually mundane procedural matters. Anything just to keep her mind awake and stop her from drifting off.

As they approached Glasgow, the dawn was breaking, and using the sat-nav in the car, they arrived at a house on the outskirts of Glasgow. It was large but not ostentatious, and although there were gates protecting the driveway, they opened automatically. No request was necessary.

Trees lined the driveway, which ran for a quarter of a mile up a small hill with the house perched looking back towards the city. The house was modern, and through the many windows, Emmett could see that a light was on. After Susan Cunningham parked the car, they all walked to the front door, but Macleod then sent Susan to the rear.

Emmett rang the doorbell, and after a few moments, they could hear someone walking down wooden stairs. The door was pulled open, and there, dressed in some casual trousers and a t-shirt, stood Orla Jones. Her hair was tatty, and she looked as if she'd been up all night, the bags under her eyes betraying her.

'Sorry to bother you, Miss Jones, but we'd like to come in and ask you a few questions.' Emmett watched her face become one of worry, but she still didn't look to be surprised by their arrival.

'This is DCI Seoras Macleod.'

'I know who the chief inspector is. I've seen him on TV,' said Orla. 'If you'll come inside, Alex is here.'

'Alex Baird?' said Emmett. And the woman nodded. 'You do know Alex Baird then.'

Orla once again nodded and pulled back the door, allowing them to enter. She closed the door behind them and asked them to follow her up a wooden staircase. This went out into an open plan on the first floor, and at the far end, by a sofa, was a man curled up tight on the floor. Emmett walked over and could see that it was Alex.

'You don't have to be here,' said Alex suddenly. 'Orla is going to sort it.'

Emmett saw Macleod raising his eyebrows at him. Emmett looked over at the wall Macleod was indicating. A ninja sword was hanging on the wall. Without being told, Sabine stepped across, and Emmett reckoned Macleod must have given her a nod in the same way. The sword was covered. Orla's path to it was blocked by Sabine.

'Won't you sit down?' said Orla. 'Alex is, well, he's a little shaken up.'

'Mr Baird has been the subject of an attack by a hitwoman out to get him. It's no wonder he's shaken up,' said Emmett.

201

'Sent by you, possibly.'

'No,' said Orla.

'You did lie, though,' said Emmett. 'Lied down in Birmingham. You said the person you saw you didn't know. You also said they had a knife inside their jacket.'

'That was a lie,' said Orla.

'And we've already had one person die down there. Alex swapped his clothing with that person. Did they tell you they made a mistake, this hitwoman?'

'I may have lied down there, but I am not lying to you now,' said Orla. 'I tell you, I have done nothing to harm Alex. Well, nothing beyond what we did at the start. We never included Alex when we made our bid to get the game produced. And when it took off, well, Steve didn't include him again. Said Alex was just a boy, said he didn't matter, and what was the twelve-year-old going to do with any of the money? He put nothing into it. We put money into it to get that initial launch. We produced the prototype.'

'But the prototype was based,' said Emmett, 'on Alex's prototype. We still have it, the original. Well, except for two dice. Two dice that Alex's father was taking, taking to talk to you.'

'No, I know nothing about Alex's father.'

'I believe,' said Emmett, 'that Alex's father took the two dice over to talk to someone who he had asked about Alex's share in the project. Asked about the fact that Alex had made the original prototype. It was Alex's game.'

'I never spoke to him. It was a terrible tragedy. I was with my folks. We were not that far away from Mellon Udrigle, but I was not there.'

'He was decapitated,' said Emmett. 'The only person capable

of that in your group would have been you. I see you still have the Oriental sword.'

'I've always carried an Oriental sword. So what?'

'Photos Alex has of you in full costume. You don't just carry a sword. You know how to use it,' said Sabine.

'I do, but I don't use it.'

'Alex was very fond of you, wasn't he?' asked Emmett.

'Yes, he was,' said Orla, 'but so was Steve. Alex was twelve. It wasn't a case of my being infatuated with him or falling for him. He was just a cute little boy. A genius with the games but a cute little boy. Steve was someone I fancied because of his ability to pull things together. He was a leader. Back then we, yes, we got close together. Back then . . .' Orla froze for a moment.

'What?' asked Emmett.

'Back then I . . . I saw Steve over at my place. He wanted the outfit for a cosplay. Friend of his. I told him to be careful with it. I told him that the sword doesn't come out of the sheath. The sword was not meant to be thrown around. He said it wouldn't be. He borrowed the outfit. It would have been around that time. It would have . . .' Ora stopped suddenly. Her hand flew to her mouth.

'Steve borrowed the sword? Steve was contacted then by Alex's dad, Mr Baird? Steve knew he was coming? Brought him to a place close by? Would have known how to decapitate someone?' asked Emmett.

Ora stood up suddenly, and walked over to the window. Tears were streaming down her eyes. 'He . . . He had asked for basic instruction. I showed him some things. I showed him how to . . . But, no. No, no, no. That's not . . .'

'That's not what?' asked Emmett.

'I didn't think. Alex had been off the books for a long while. We'd gone ahead; Alex had been left behind. I never thought that, well, when Alex's father died, I didn't think that it was anything to do with us. I didn't see. I didn't!'

'No one really did, but that was his way of handling it,' said Emmett. 'He would have gone quietly. He wouldn't have kicked up a fuss. He'd have tried to sort it out and be reasonable. But I'm guessing he never got a chance.'

Orla was now white. She was looking across at Alex. Suddenly, she ran over and knelt down, put her arms around his head, and started to kiss him, like a mother kisses a baby. 'I'm so sorry, I'm so sorry, I . . .'

'Alex said something at the start,' said Macleod suddenly, 'about you sorting it all out. You were going to do that by . . .'

The woman looked up suddenly, her eyes fearful. 'I phoned Steve. I told Steve that Alex was here. Said it was time to make amends for the game. We had to give Alex his due. I said . . .'

'How long ago did you say this?' asked Macleod.

'Just over an hour,' she said. 'Just over an hour.'

Macleod grabbed his mobile. He placed a call to Susan Cunningham, telling her to get around to the front door and to come inside. He marched down the stairs, leaving Emmett and Sabine with Alex and Orla. Together, Susan and Macleod went round the house, making sure every door was locked, every window sealed. Then he placed a call to the local constabulary, asking for assistance. Within half an hour there were police cars around the building, but he did not let anyone in. After he called the constabulary, he placed another call to a woman he now thought of as a friend.

* * *

A green motorbike pulled up at the service station, parked at the pump, and then the rider turned to check the pannier on the back of the motorbike. As she did so, she was watched by another woman in a car on the edge of the forecourt. Quietly, the woman in the car inserted something into her mouth. It was held delicately on the tip of her tongue, and the tongue curled around it, holding it. She closed her mouth, and then, seeing that the biker had removed her helmet, she stepped out of the car.

For a moment she stopped, watching the biker scan the forecourt. Then, with the helmet now sitting on the pannier, the biker took hold of one of the fuel dispensers, lifted it off its cradle, and turned to fuel up her bike.

The woman from the car casually walked over towards the pump. Although she was wearing boots, they made no sound. This was partly because of the way she walked, and not just their design. The woman who was filling up the bike didn't notice the woman from the car until she was within five feet.

At this point, the woman from the bike heard something, shook the handle of the dispenser, let the trigger go, cutting the fuel supply, and placed the handle back in the cradle. As she turned to do it, the woman from the car walked past. There was an almost imperceptible noise as the woman blew through her encircled tongue and fired the object she had placed in her mouth.

There was a sudden realisation from the woman on the bike, a momentary gaze, the eyes of one professional to another, and then the woman on the bike slumped. Quickly, the woman from the car dropped and checked the vitals of the woman on the ground. She shook her. She made sure that the woman on the ground was not getting back up. And then she hurried inside the garage to the kiosk, where an assistant was looking out through the window in horror.

'Is she okay?'

'I'm just phoning an ambulance,' said the woman from the car. 'I thought it's safer in here. Not meant to use phones on a forecourt, are you?'

'No, no.'

After placing the call, the woman from the car walked out back to the woman on the ground, followed by the assistant. Another car pulled in, and a man anxiously watched the woman on the ground. The woman from the car, however, was unfazed, explaining to the man that the woman had collapsed and an ambulance was on its way.

The ambulance arrived five minutes later and, if both the onlookers had seriously thought about it, it was an incredibly rapid response for an ambulance. Two paramedics jumped out quickly, assessed the woman, got her onto a stretcher and put her in the back of the ambulance before driving away. The woman from the car received the thanks of the assistant, but when asked her name, failed to give an answer, instead explaining about how she had seen a situation like this before. It was only when the woman had driven off that the assistant realised she had no details.

Later that day, if anyone who owned the petrol station had gone to look at the CCTV of the forecourt and tried to identify the woman—either on the bike or the woman who had been in the car—they would have failed. Strangely, that time period was missing.

The woman from the car, one Anna Hunt, head of the Service, had smiled as she drove several minutes behind the ambulance. It never went to any hospital. Instead, it pulled into a farmhouse, specifically into a barn at the side. Anna, however, pulled her car into the driveway, marched in through the front door of the house, upstairs and into a room which contained only one seat. In that seat, the woman from the bike was now sitting, although she was tied to it with very up to date and secure restraints.

Anna stood watching her, for the woman hadn't yet come round. Outside the door of the room, some members of her Service would be watching, protecting, and giving Anna the time to talk to the woman when she came to. She had only one more thing to do before that interview. She sent a message. It was simple. It said, 'She is no threat.'

Chapter 25

'It's not like you to have everyone round.'

'I was told it was an instruction,' said Emmett.

'Instruction?'

'Yes, Macleod said to me, "You need to have a wrap-up. When you get to the bottom of the case, you have a wrap-up. Clarissa takes her lot out. He always has something for a big case, and says Hope will do it too. Says it doesn't matter that there aren't that many of us involved in the case, that it needs to be done.'

'And so you just invited everybody round here?'

'It seemed appropriate,' said Emmett. 'No point going out somewhere is there? I mean. Macleod's not a big party man. Perry's not really either. Susan yes, maybe—you're not. I'm not; nobody else really to invite.'

'You could have brought round the rest of them.'

'No. Macleod said no. It was the cold-case team, anybody that worked with us. Susan got involved there at the end, Perry was involved with us, Macleod, you and me. We're a small team; it's the way we are, so we have a small venue, my house.'

'And so what, you decided to cook for us all?'

'Why not,' said Emmett. 'I can cook. I'm not just bringing a

208

takeaway in. I thought I would do it properly. People would then see that I'm making an effort.'

'Do you not always make an effort? Nobody sits thinking you're not making an effort.'

'I did a bit of research though. They always go out for curry. Big on a curry at the end of a case—the other ones—so I thought I'd make one.'

Sabine saw all the pots, pans, and the like around the kitchen. The smell was wonderful. She'd never realised that Emmett could cook.

'You've made nothing like this for me.'

'When you come round, it's not about eating, is it?' he said. 'It's about playing the games. Taking part? We have that different about us. This is work. When you come around, it's not work. At least, I hope it's not work. It's something beyond work, isn't it?'

Sabine smiled. Part of her felt she was blushing. She had thought about coming around that night, wearing something fancy. Wearing something that would have reached out to the very male side of Emmett. Something that might have stirred something else in him. But that's not what Emmett would have wanted, she'd thought.

And so, she was wearing her jeans and her t-shirt. Yes, it was a T-shirt with an enormous dragon on it, but it was just a T-shirt. She had done little with her hair either, simply brushed it, and because she wasn't working, it wasn't up in its traditional ponytail. When she'd arrived, he had smiled broadly, but there was nothing unusual in that, or anything indicating more. It was maybe the thing that frustrated her, but was he just shy or was she just on the wrong end of the stick?

When she thought he was in trouble—when she'd run into

the house in Birmingham after she had taken on the hitwoman and she thought he might not be alive in there—she had kissed him, passionately, gratefully, and Emmett hadn't responded. He had done nothing. He'd just got on with the case. There were no words for her about it. He hadn't said anything to her about it. Deep inside, Sabine wondered if she'd got this wrong. Was he just someone who liked her on a platonic level?

Sabine was all for having platonic friends, but she was someone who needed someone. Not everyone did, and she didn't need someone to run riot with physically. No, she wanted more than that. It wasn't just the physical side of things she wanted. She wanted to be close to someone, but not just as a friend. Ultimately, she still needed a lover. She wondered if Emmett did too, or was he just not that way inclined?

'Stir that over there,' he said. A few moments later, the doorbell rang, and Emmett opened it up to Macleod, who'd arrived with a bottle of wine. He clearly did not know about wine, but regardless, it was appreciated, and when Perry and Susan then turned up, conversation seemed to flow easily. Perry was good at it although Emmett thought Susan Cunningham was quite quiet.

The team ate together, and conversation flowed about the case. They talked about how they weren't sure what would stick against Steve Dingle. Would the murder conviction stick? Certainly, he would get stung for having stolen an idea. Alex, and Majik Falls. Steve had been the one to push it and take it on. Orla had admitted fault in going along with it. And the others had too. But that would get bogged down in legal wrangles.

First was a re-look into the case of the murder of Martin Baird. The first interview with Steve Dingle had been one where he said nothing. But then, when he realised Orla had said she'd lent her sword, he'd panicked. The sword was the same one. Could they match up the cut? Forensics weren't sure, but they would continue to work on it.

There were questions to be asked about where he was that night. But Steve Dingle had good legal representation. And Macleod wasn't sure just what would stick and what wouldn't. There'd be months of working alongside the authorities to see what they could do to convict the man properly. On the other hand, Macleod had pointed out that the key threat to Alex's life had been quashed.

That was the other side. What Anna Hunt knew, and what could Anna Hunt bring to the party? Macleod hadn't heard from her yet. No doubt she was debriefing the hired killer. But when she was done, what could she give to a court? Macleod was hopeful, if not guaranteeing, that Anna would give good information.

Emmett noted throughout the meal, however, that Perry and Susan were sitting on opposite sides of the table. There was definite awkwardness between them. He thought it must be hard, difficult for them to get along. And he told Sabine so. He told Sabine this as the dishes were being brought out to the kitchen. And all Sabine could think about was the fact he said nothing about her and him.

After the dishes were done, and the five of them returned to the living room, Emmett disappeared into a back room. He then told them to come through to another room, which contained a large table. There were drink holders at certain parts of the table and a board had been placed on the table, laid out in the middle. There were five places, five sets of dice. Emmett asked if any of them would want to sit anywhere in particular, and he named the five classes of character within the game. Macleod caught on quickly, recognising it.

'Majik Falls. This is the game it was all about. This is what he invented.'

'Yes,' said Emmett. 'I thought we should give it a go.'

Macleod shook his head but Sabine told him to sit down. 'You don't know what you're missing,' she said.

Perry was bemused. But soon, within half an hour, there were arguments and debates going on about the game. They played for hours, Emmett in his element, Sabine watching him, seeing how he enjoyed it all. But she was more surprised by how Macleod got into it. Was he enjoying it, or was he indulging Emmett? She couldn't tell.

Perry and Susan seemed at ease playing it, although they were clearly collaborating. Maybe it helped with the awkwardness they felt at still working together.

Working together. Emmett and I are still working together. So, clearly, there's nothing going on. Nothing he wants. As the game finished, Sabine sighed and walked through to the kitchen. She was soon joined by Perry.

'Well, that was interesting,' he said. 'Never played one of those. I thought I did well.'

'You won,' said Sabine. 'Though you had some help.'

'Yes, Susan was quite kind. It's not been easy. But she seems to have accepted it. I had to decide,' said Perry. 'Honestly, I had to stop dragging everyone along and just decide. I had to ask the question of myself and then of Tanya. You have to take positive action. You have to be in charge of what's going on. Can't just let it drift along.'

'Are you talking about yourself or are you talking to me, Perry?'

Perry put on a shocked face. 'I don't offer advice. I take Macleod's tack. Don't offer advice. Keep out of it.'

'And just make random statements that we're all meant to suck in.'

'I'm detecting jealousy because you lost the game, despite the fact you've been playing an awful lot of these games,' said Perry. Sabine smiled. 'That,' said Perry, 'is a loaded statement. Right, I need to go. I'll drop the boss man off. Are you needing a lift?'

'I could do with one, yes. Yes, I could.' Ten minutes later, everyone had their coats and were heading out to the car. Perry was going to take Susan, Macleod and Sabine home. When they all got to the door, Sabine was almost the last to leave. As she did so, she turned to give Emmett a hug. She kissed him on the cheek. But as she turned to follow the others out to the car, she felt a hand grab hold of hers. 'I'll give you a lift home,' Emmett said.

'Why?' asked Sabine.

'I'll give you a lift home.'

She smiled at him, then turned and ran after the others. Explaining briefly that Emmett wanted some help, she then went back to the house, knowing that none of them would believe her. When she got there, she was slightly surprised because Emmett had his coat on and was indeed taking her to his car. Once there, they drove in silence back to Sabine's rented flat.

'Here we go,' he said.

'Yes,' she said. 'I'm here.'

There was silence for a moment, and Sabine was angry. *If he just would say something, if he would just . . .* 'Good night, Emmett,' she said, opening the car door and preparing to exit.

213

But a hand shot across, grabbing her wrist.

'When you kissed me,' he said, 'that wasn't just relief. That was . . .'

'Yes, it was,' said Sabine. 'If that's not how you feel, that's fine. I know you're different, know you don't react that way. I know you're looking for friends. Hell Emmett, I know . . .'

Emmett pulled her suddenly close and kissed her, almost roughly. Then he stopped. 'I do,' he said, 'but I don't know how, and I don't know if we can.'

Sabine sat back in her seat. 'We can! Whether we should is another matter,' she said. 'Do you want to come in and talk about it?'

He was almost trembling as she looked at him. 'Not right now,' he said. 'Not right now.'

Part of Sabine felt hurt, but another part was looking at Emmett. He'd gone out of his way. What he'd just done for him was enormous.

'Whenever you're ready,' said Sabine. She leant forward and kissed him again on the cheek. Her hand went up, and tussled his hair. 'Just know that I'm always ready.'

She stepped out of the car, went to her door, and noticed he watched her all the way until she was safe inside. Sabine felt giddy and, strangely, lost. She'd stepped out, and she did not know where she stood, no idea who this man was. She'd been with him, she'd played his games, she'd worked alongside him, and still Emmett Grump was a mystery. But it was her mystery to solve, and solve it she would.

Read on to discover the Patrick Smythe series!

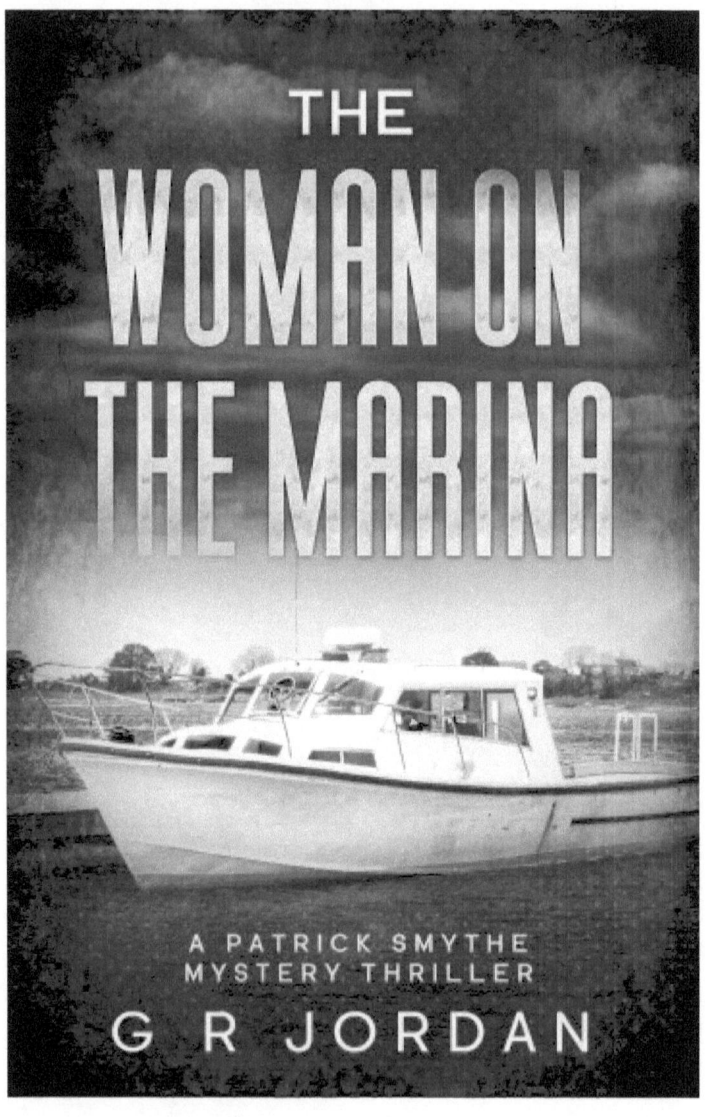

THE
WOMAN ON
THE MARINA

A PATRICK SMYTHE
MYSTERY THRILLER

G R JORDAN

Patrick Smythe is a former Northern Irish policeman who

after suffering an amputation after a bomb blast, takes to the sea between the west coast of Scotland and his homeland to ply his trade as a private investigator. Join Paddy as he tries to work to his own ethics while knowing how to bend the rules he once enforced. Working from his beloved motorboat 'Craigantlet', Paddy decides to rescue a drug mule in this short story from the pen of G R Jordan.

Join G R Jordan's monthly newsletter about forthcoming releases and special writings for his tribe of avid readers and then receive your free Patrick Smythe short story.

Go to https://bit.ly/PatrickSmythe for your Patrick Smythe journey to start

About the Author

GR Jordan is a self-published author who finally decided at forty that in order to have an enjoyable lifestyle, his creative beast within would have to be unleashed. His books mirror that conflict in life where acts of decency contend with self-promotion, goodness stares in horror at evil, and kindness blindsides us when we at our worst. Corrupting our world with his parade of wondrous and horrific characters, he highlights everyday tensions with fresh eyes whilst taking his methodical, intelligent mainstays on a roller-coaster ride of dilemmas, all the while suffering the banter of their provocative sidekicks.

A graduate of Loughborough University where he masqueraded as a chemical engineer but ultimately played American football, Gary had worked at changing the shape of cereal flakes and pulled a pallet truck for a living. Watching vegetables freeze at -40'C was another career highlight and he was also one of the Scottish Highlands "blind" air traffic controllers.

These days he has graduated to answering a telephone to people in trouble before telephoning other people to sort it out.

Having flirted with most places in the UK, he is now based in the Isle of Lewis in Scotland where his free time is spent between raising a young family with his wife, writing, figuring out how to work a loom and caring for a small flock of chickens. Luckily, his writing is influenced by his varied work and life experience as the chickens have not been the poetical inspiration he had hoped for!

You can connect with me on:

🌐 https://grjordan.com

📘 https://facebook.com/carpetlessleprechaun

Subscribe to my newsletter:

✉ https://bit.ly/PatrickSmythe

Also by G R Jordan

G R Jordan writes across multiple genres including crime, dark and action adventure fantasy, feel good fantasy, mystery thriller and horror fantasy. Below is a selection of his work. Whilst all books are available across online stores, signed copies are available at his personal shop.

 **The Academy for Murder (Highlands & Islands Detective Book 48)**
https://grjordan.com/product/the-academy-for-murder
The murder of a Headmistress. An embittered and frightened staff room. In a private school of over three hundred can Macleod find the pupil who really doesn't like their teachers?

The brutal murder of the Headmistress of the Applecross Academy for the Gifted brings Macleod and his team to the rural west of Scotland. In a whirlpool of egos and reputations, the team must shift out the strongest feelings that would cause such anger and barbarity in an intellectual haven. As the DCI unearths scandal and intrigue, he finds the veneer of the school peeling and suspects aplenty. Can Macleod give the school a lesson in detection, or will he be bettered by those of a higher intellect?

Corporal punishment is no thing of the past!

Kirsten Stewart Thrillers
https://grjordan.com/product/a-shot-at-democracy

Join Kirsten Stewart on a shadowy ride through the underbelly of the Highlands of Scotland where among the beauty and splendour of the majestic landscape lies corruption and intrigue to match any city. From murders to extortion, missing children to criminals operating above the law, the Highland former detective must learn a tougher edge to her work as she puts her own life on the line to protect those who cannot defend themselves.

Having left her beloved murder investigation team far behind, Kirsten has to battle personal tragedy and loss while adapting to a whole new way of executing her duties where your mistakes are your own. As Kirsten comes to terms with working with the new team, she often operates as the groups solo field agent, placing herself in danger and trouble to rescue those caught on the dark side of life. With action packed scenes and tense scenarios of murder and greed, the Kirsten Stewart thrillers will have you turning page after page to see your favourite Scottish lass home!

There's life after Macleod, but a whole new world of death!

Jac's Revenge (A Jac Moonshine Thriller #1)

https://grjordan.com/product/jacs-revenge

An unexpected hit makes Debbie a widow. The attention of her man's killer spawns a brutal yet classy alter ego. But how far can you play the game before it takes over your life?

All her life, Debbie Parlor lived in her man's shadow, knowing his work was never truly honest. She turned her head from news stories and rumours. But when he was disposed of for his smile to placate a rival crime lord, Jac Moonshine was born. And when Debbie is paid compensation for her loss like her car was written off, Jac decides that enough is enough.

Get on board with this tongue-in-cheek revenge thriller that will make you question how far you would go to avenge a loved one, and how much you would enjoy it!

A Giant Killing (Siobhan Duffy Mysteries #1)
https://grjordan.com/product/a-giant-killing
A body lies on the Giant's boot. Discord, as the master of secrets has been found. Can former spy Siobhan Duffy find the killer before they execute her former colleagues?

When retired operative Siobhan Duffy sees the killing of her former master in the paper, her unease sends her down a path of discovery and fear. Aided by her young housekeeper and scruff of a gardener, Siobhan begins a quest to discover the reason for her spy boss' death and unravels a can of worms today's masters would rather keep closed. But in a world of secrets, the difference between revenge and simple, if brutal, housekeeping becomes the hardest truth to know.

The past is a child who never leaves home!

www.ingramcontent.com/pod-product-compliance
Lightning Source LLC
Chambersburg PA
CBHW060545190726
48283CB00003B/876